Ancient Realms II

AWAKENED

by Samuel F. McCord

Ancientrealmsll@yahoo.com

Chapters

Introduction - Biographical

This book will start as a biography, at the beginning and throughout my younger years of life, to introduce to you the true nature of our being, purpose in life and the unlimited potential that we all have. I will discuss our origins as spiritual beings to the natural spiritual laws that we are governed by. I will give you instructions on how to achieve every psychic ability known to man and why psychic abilities are simply the natural progression of one's soul's awakening. From here, with increased awakening, one will surpass the psychic abilities, which will become second nature to you and your true soul will be awakened to the realms of our ancient nature – of oneness or Christ-consciousness.

Allow me to begin when I was a youngster of twelve years. This is about the time when I first started to realize that I was a little bit different from my friends. I had always felt, and seen other people, or forms, most people refer to them as ghosts. I had always assumed that everybody felt and saw, what I saw. I asked one of my friends one day when we were having a sleep over, "Did you see that one, it's really big, black and grey looking?" He said, "What?" "What are you looking at?" I said, "That ghost figure." I couldn't believe my friend couldn't see it. He stared at me for a few seconds, and said, "You're weird," and turned around, and he went back to playing. I didn't believe him, so I asked my other friends, "Do you see it?" I got the same reactions. They all thought I was joking. That was the first one that scared me a bit.

With them that's when I realized, that others just couldn't see, what I saw. From then on, I didn't say much to anybody else, until I reached high school, and had more time to research some of these subjects.

The only other time I asked about it, was when I went to church.

I was raised in a Lutheran Church by my parents. I forget exactly what age I was between eight and ten years old, but I know it was before I had catechism training in Church, or close to that time. Two years prior to my completion of catechism training on almost every Sunday, I would question what I was being taught. The main questions that I remember asking over and over were-----"How do you know what heaven looks like, and where is it?" "Where do you go when, you go to heaven or hell?""How was man, created?" "What is the devil?" "How do you know reincarnation isn't real?" I asked, myself, "If re-incarnation isn't real, then what am I seeing with ghosts?" "Why do you have only one life to get all of these things right?" (There was a lot to "get right," and I had already made my share of mistakes). "Why isn't everybody a pastor, or priest?" "Why do we have several types of religions, if there is only one God?" "Doesn't that create problems between was different to me and it would simply be another type of "psychic ability," that they were describing.

Upon graduation from high school, I chose to go to college. Once, in my second year at that college, I showed one of my roommates how I could draw a symbol on a piece of paper, light it on fire, and the fire would burn everything, except the symbol. The fire simply made a circle around it, and burned out, never touching the symbol. He was fascinated at first, because he couldn't find the words to describe how "Eerie," he felt about me. It was simply a joke for me to freak him out, because we were talking about ghosts that night. The next day; however, he suddenly called me "a witch," and others joined in on the name calling and just started to stay away from me. It was a good lesson one of many to come that I have learned there is a time and place when to show and not show and when to say and not say things.

Remember, your mind is your builder the creator. What you think - will become your reality. Nothing ever happens physically, unless it has run through your mind, first and foremost. The physical is the end result, or manifestation of the physical. I can't impress and stress this enough to you.

Meditation – Regular and Trans-meditation

Let's start with some simple basics first. Good points you can use for anything else in this book that I'm going to describe and have you do in this book. Let's call them building blocks to everything else.

Regular meditation was what I first learned from books, and it did work for me. It was, so far as I knew, all there was to meditation. So I began to experiment and explore other approaches to trans-meditation to cover questions that continued to drive my need for more learning. So I soon found my own methods using trans-meditation that I was learning worked more efficiently, and within months information and answers started to flow in that I had questions on, but I didn't yet understand what was going on with the questions. Just that it was cool. Once I figured out kinda of what was going on then I started to understand the process of channeling information.

Now I have opened a gate for information to flow in. Again, I thought that was pretty cool. Didn't understand how, but was cool. Now the gate was wide open and I didn't know or understand how to close it or slow it down. So now the information was coming to me while i was fully conscious and doing any activity. At work, driving, eating, at the store and etc.

In those early attempts the information I received was completely random on every subject imaginable. Anytime, whether, day or night I would receive information about a multitude of subjects. It was rarely on the same topic. On occasion, it would be on reincarnation, and the very next moment, it would be how to use psychic abilities, more efficiently and the origins of our beings. I never knew what was going to come up or when.

I was always surprised at what I was going to learn or receive. For two years I carried around pads of paper to write this information down, because I was afraid that I was going to forget the information given. Little did I know, "I would not," forget it! Whenever I needed it, it was brought forward to me, like a filing system in a library, but I still continued to write it all down, just in case it would disappear on me.

When I would write this information down, I could barely write it down fast enough to catch all of the words. Sometimes, it flowed with only two or three sentences, and at other times, I would write down pages of information. Sometimes, it was easy to understand and write down, at other times, it was given in language similar to, as The Bible, reads----which definitely slowed me down, when trying to write in detail. Sometimes I would get information that I could not explain to myself; not to mention, thinking: "How do I even explain this to others?" I can't even explain or understand this myself.

In a couple of years, I learned how to control this flow, and when and where, and even if, I wanted the information or wait until later. I had built up so much information. I also learned that I could ask myself a question, and then, "boom," the answer would be there. Some information (the more advanced information) I would receive it, and then come to understand it later on within days to weeks and sometimes months.

Once I clearly understood the information given to me, new information would come to me right where I left off, and it would advance me even further, just as if, I was reading a book. I was amazed, and most of the information made common everyday sense. Of course, I questioned "the how," "the what," and "could the information," be trusted? I tested the information over so many times to test its accuracy. I never kept track as in a book or notebook, but my sayings to others and every ability I chose to use is somewhere in the ninety-eight to ninety-nine percentile accurate. Plus over the many decades now it's generally very accurate. Even my father had tested me quite a bit. Being a police officer for 41 years and a detective for most of it he was very skeptical, but became a believer. He did realize there are people out there that are genuine, but very rare in his opinion. A lot of fakes and gypsies he would call them.

Now let me describe how I used to meditate in the beginning for you. This method does work and there are also a lot of books out there on meditation that go in a lot more detail than I do. I start with finding a quiet and comfortable place I like in my house. I sit down on the floor and cross my legs. I used to hold my hands together as if I was praying to keep my energy inside flowing in a circular motion. Later on I always kept my hands separate from each other and close to where my knees are positioned and eventually they rise upwards. I close my eyes and see all of the things that went on for the day go through my mind. One thought at a time, I dismiss or clear each thought from my mind and letting them go.

From here I realized I could listen to the inside of my physical body. It would have creaks, tweaks and flows that you can hear within your body. This is how you become sensitive to listening to your body. I would say this is the first step you should try to understand and complete with meditation. It will help you clear your mind, relax and teach yourself how to focus.

As for my experiences with practicing trans-mediation---I found the only differences from regular meditation were mainly in using visualizations. I found that combining visualization and imagery to my meditation that I had more control over everything I wanted to do. With trans-meditation you meditate as I mentioned above, but then with imagery you can imagine moving your blood flow around in your body to areas that need more attention. If your body is in pain, you start to imagine this area of pain disappearing or becoming numb to your senses so you no longer feel the pain. Or move more blood flow to an injured area of yours. I will give more detailed information on healing your pains in my healing chapters. In meditation you are simply relaxing your thoughts and your body.

Another thing you can do with trans-mediation is empty your mind so you can project questions outwards from your body, while leaving your mind empty. With your mind empty answers will just simply pop in there out of nowhere. like a light build type of answer or solution. These answers are the accurate ones. To test this information, the information received is generally answered in a way outside of how you talk normally. It is as if somebody is talking to you and the answers aren't coming from your own thoughts. Or it could just be an idea that just "pops" into your head.

Or you could project your thoughts out to others to help them as in prayer, but more direct to the person or even out to the weather or the general population. After you clear your thoughts, you imagine one thought that you would like to project, create or send to others. Then you visualize that image or message projecting from yourself, out to whomever or whatever you have in mind. It is very effective. I guess you can call it a vibrational email.

As I continued to advance and receive more and more information in these practices---I soon discovered, oneness, and oneness turned out to be the most efficient method, as well as, a gateway to all of my acquired "psychic abilities." For someone starting out, you must experiment with your own ways to be able to understand oneness. It would be like seeing a car for the first time and someone saying, "Drive it." You are not sure what the car is, not to mention, how to turn it on, and steer it. So I would recommend starting out with the "Tried and True," method of regular meditation first and then on to trans-meditation. Then learn your body and try channeling. From here, you can try oneness. I describe how you can achieve oneness in my next chapter, but if you have not meditated before, I highly recommend it first, to get used to it. Oneness can and will open up a lot of doors for you. It's better to ease into it than try to crash course into it. If you try to crash course oneness, you could spend years trying to get it organized and under control.

I am going to re-iterate the method of meditation again in more detail. Try to pick a quiet and comfortable place for you to begin, at first. You'll want an area and a time frame when you know you won't have many distractions. You should only need around ten minutes. Your goal at first is to get comfortable with your physical body. Once you find yourself a good area, you should sit on the floor, or in a comfortable chair, in any way that is as relaxing as possible for you. Just don't get too relaxed, and let yourself fall asleep. First, take a few deep breaths and exhale, similar to sighs. This helps you get some fresh oxygen into your body, and actually helps your body to relax. That is why people will sigh during the day not a yawn; it's a defense mechanism that your body does to help it get a quick jolt of relaxation, and calm down in regards to any stress you might feel. Your mind will be full of your daily thoughts you have had throughout the day (and there will be quite a few). One by one, imagine them just disappearing, or imagine them flying away, until your down to just one thought of yourself meditating. Picture yourself sitting there with your eyes closed, and nobody else around, just you in silence. Concentrate on your peacefulness, and the stillness.

Now listen and feel yourself breathing. Feel the air come into your body, and gently exiting from your body. Just sit there and imagine your solitude, and envision it with your mind, for a minute or two. Get comfortable with it. Don't try to control it. Relax---practice this before you proceed any further. It may take you several times of trying. Don't fight it. As they say, "Go with the flow," and "Take it easy." Then try to clear your mind of thoughts. As you become more practiced, your breathing will automatically start to slow down. Let your breathing slow down. Relax, concentrate. If you have gotten this far, you are already meditating to a small degree, and your mind and body will like it.

By clearing your mind, you are releasing the stress and tension of the day. Just remember, stress is generally caused by our own thoughts of what we feel is a nuisance or annoying. A perception of what is uncomfortable to you. Think of it this way. Either you can accomplish the task at hand, or you can't. Either way, if it is the best that you can do, then don't worry about it. You will get better at accepting it. It may take some time. Your stress levels will be much lower through practicing meditation, and that's a good thing for you as a person. A lot of cancers are brought on by stress. Remember, mind is the physical creator---the physical is the end result of that building. Create stress in your mind, and your physical body will eventually show its effect.

Okay, let's take you into a much deeper meditation. We need to get you to where you are imagining your lungs in your head, and feeling them inhale and exhale; expand and contract. This needs to be the only thought in your mind. Let's now listen to your heart once again. See and feel it pumping, and slowing down. Imagine your heart pounding with blood coming in and going out. Let's take it a step further. After seeing and feeling your heart pumping naturally, imagine your blood exiting your heart, and traveling to the rest of your body. See and feel your blood flowing to your arms, legs, stomach, and brain. See it branch out to all parts of you, like with a tree and its branches. Put the image in your mind, and feel the image in your body, in this normal state of being.

If you concentrate too much on your arms, or spend more time in one area than another, your mind can actually push and/or retain more blood to those areas. So you want to try to keep it equal throughout. Just take several minutes and feel the natural flow of your body. At this point, you will also hear and feel little creaks and movements in your physique. When you do this, it's the first level of realizing what you feel inside of your body. You are now becoming more sensitive to yourself physically. This is good. This is also the first stage of how you start to learn about how to diagnose yourself physically. We'll discuss more of this subject later on when we cover the possibility of you being able to heal yourself and others.

Now you have achieved sensitivity to your body, it is time to go back to your thoughts. This is where you now have several options, from which to choose. You can go further and try to become one with yourself, and everything around you (Oneness). You can try to receive information openly (you should have a specific question in mind as it works better that way), start to heal and/or diagnose yourself, ask yourself questions about anything (as long as your intention is honest and forthright). Travel outside your body, pick up on other people's thoughts, or just try to review your past lives, and other's lives, if you can recall them at this point. Whatever you choose, you must specifically think about it, one thought at a time. If your mind wanders (which it will in the beginning), then try to start over, or wait for another day or period of time, until you can relax and concentrate.

You have plenty of time, because time is of no use to you, during these experiences. Taking the action is what is important, and that action will follow you in other lives. The best responses and answers come to you when you keep that one thought; seeing and feeling it move forward, only by itself. It will take some practice to get to this point.

Some people can pick it up very fast, while others are a bit slower. Those that have more fears, in general, or are more skeptical, will be slower. Fear in general is a big huge block to experience. Skeptic's actually block knowledge, wisdom, and experience, which creates no advancement of seeing what others can see. They expect first before experiencing. You block yourself from remembering and seeing anything outside of the physical realm. Remember, there is nothing on the Earth, or in our galaxy to fear. If you want to progress in spirituality and psychic abilities, one of the main ingredients in oneness is releasing your fears of (eventually) everything. Fear is wasteful and very draining.

From physical sensitivity, the next step is the mental aspect. Anything you choose to know, or try to do or accomplish, is through concentrating on just one thought. Remember, everything that manifests itself in the physical, has manifested itself in your thoughts first. Clear your mind of your thoughts down to one, and constantly concentrate on that one image of what you want to achieve, and eventually, see it as a completed or achieved result, in the physical sense. For example, if you want an answer, imagine your question leaving your body and going upwards or outwards. Then, with patience feel that question as an answer coming back to yourself. Do not let your conscious mind have the pre-determined answer. Leave your mind blank and empty. Just let the answer, appear or, “pop,” into your mind, similar to inspiration. If the answer doesn’t come it just might when you wake up in the morning. Some answers come later on instead of directly to you in that moment.

There is a big difference between your conscious thoughts and your ideas. For example, when that light bulb (idea) just appears over your head or when an idea suddenly comes to you. Once you get this down then try oneness if you choose to expand further in your spiritual awakening.

In conclusion use and try meditation in your life, even if it is only for a few minutes each day. It could help you immensely in life. Even if it only helps your body and mind through calmness. So I would recommend in this order - Meditation, trans-meditation, then become sensitive to listening and understanding your body, then try channeling with questions. After all that then you can try oneness.

Introduction of Oneness

Oneness touches upon everything! It is the key to unlimited potential. Oneness can be used for anything, whether it is physical (sports), the mind, subjects of interest, or learning, or in spiritual growth or psychic abilities. If you want to push yourself to the limit, and achieve the maximum benefit, you must utilize oneness. Have you ever heard somebody, say, "be one with the ball," or "be one with your car?" They are talking about the mental degree of oneness. By becoming as one with your ball, as in sports, or your car, as in racing, you are visualizing that ball from your hit to the hole or goal line. You see it, before you have even reacted to it physically. Like a golfer is visualizing the path that he wants the ball to go in before hitting it. In racing you become one with your car. You're completely focused on the track and your car mimics your thoughts of what you want it to do. You can feel every creak, tweak and noise your car is making and can act appropriately to push or not push your car to your goal.

My own definition of oneness (in the physical and mental, aspect) is, when your mind concentrates solely (at least at first), on one objective. You start "To See," the objective through imagery, then you feel that objective, then you become one with your goal or objective, this is oneness. Mind is the builder---the physical is the end result. Oneness is achieved by keeping conscious control of your surroundings, yet you still become synchronized with the objective, you can then become the objective.

When I was younger, like I had mentioned earlier, I started out with basic meditation. It did work, but by adding imagery, I went further and obtained oneness. I didn't even know at the time what it was, and it really surprised me at first. After a couple of months of practicing trans-meditation for about twenty minutes a day, I realized my visualizations had taken me outside my own body, while my physical body was sitting on the carpet. At first, it didn't really sink in. I didn't understand. Then I remembered reading about astral travel. When I finally got my mind around that, I was completely amazed at the results I could do with it. One second I could be astral traveling and then, "boom," the next second I was back in my body opening my eyes.

Several days later, I felt my body floating again thinking I'm astral traveling. I opened my eyes, and saw that the ceiling was much closer than it usually is. I looked down and saw the floor several feet beneath me, and then I was surprised again, and I fell to the floor. This time, instead of astral traveling, I had levitated my body, but the feeling was the same.

A couple of weeks later, I was meditating and my body felt strange. Strange all over, as if my physical body was gone----vanished, just my mind and my thoughts were all that I could sense. I opened my eyes, and everything appeared to be the same----no floating and my body was still here. I didn't notice it at first, but when I looked down again to make sure I was sitting on the ground, I noticed my legs were gone, and parts of my arms were disappearing going in and out of shape. Once again, I felt I was losing control of myself, and within less than a second, "boom," I was just sitting there on the floor looking at my legs and arms, as if nothing had happened.

I soon found myself getting used to these happenings. So I began trying it again with the main purpose, each time, of getting that strange feeling that I had again. It took a couple of times, and then it was happening again. I felt compelled to get up and move around this time with my eyes open. So I stood up, but it seemed to take several seconds to get up, even though it appeared to take the same amount of time as usual. When I stood up that strange feeling still remained. So I decided to walk around the house a little bit to see if I would keep it, or lose that feeling. The feeling still remained.

But, what was so different was that all of my movements were as if I were in a slow motion video, and yet, I knew that I was moving in the typical manner and speed as usual, and that was what made it so strange to me. Then I stopped and realized that my body was blending into everything around me. The air, floor, furniture, and every step I took was being mixed together with the floor. Everything moved in harmony and balance with each other, while having a weird kind of respect going on, at the same time. This was my first realization of what true oneness was in the spiritual aspect.

I must warn you of some consequences of oneness. If you so choose, to try to attempt oneness in this manner, or even choose to progress re-learning of your roots, or psychic abilities, the first time you ever really achieve oneness, you will never see life the same way again. You will start to realize what the physical three dimensional world really is, an illusion and what the third dimension (the physical world we live in) has to offer to all of us.

It will permanently change your life forever, and throughout, your future lives. All of your pre-conceived notions about life and its meanings will change. It would be, for example, when somebody has a near death experience, afterwards they seem to be a little bit changed from that point on, in their views of life in general. Every moment counts from that point on. It will be hard to have normal conversations or with co-workers at that point because they will complain about this or that or gossip and to you you will no longer quite see your surroundings as being problems and no need to talk down to another and etc.

Oneness is like that, except you will have a slightly different understanding and experience of what you truly are as a person, and your purpose in the scheme of life, as a whole. For example, you will start to understand how every grain of sand is about a chain reaction. You see, you affect your surroundings or pieces of sand around you. Then the surrounding sand affects their surrounding pieces of sand and so on. Like a wave in the ocean traveling along the surface. Everything and everybody, affects everything and everybody in the world. No matter how insignificant you feel you are from a doctor in a big city to a homeless person on the street. The wave of vibration travels in and through everything. You can actually consciously blend into it all with oneness.

If oneness is achieved even temporarily in your life, you will never look at life the same again. You will never look at life as just working a 9 to 5 job, having a family and just running through the motions of physical life. You will see that the motions of physical life is not important at all with all of its made up drama. You will see, feel and know that something bigger is actually behind it all and we are connected together as one big family. Once you experience oneness you can never undue it. Yes, you can live a normal life and such, but that experience and knowledge that comes with it will never be lost. It becomes a part of you forever. Kinda of like ignorance is bliss saying because you're no longer ignorant after that point. Maybe this is where religion came up with the saying of eating the forbidden fruit in the Garden of Eden? Perhaps they didn't understand what oneness is really about?

Karma is our safety net for our spiritual awakening. In awakening to our karma, growing closer – step by step- closer to our origins, back to God. This growth will be individual, as well as collective, and can be shared by all.

Every action you do has an effect on us and others around us. We judge ourselves through our soul and compare it to the golden rules. If our intentions were incorrect compared to the golden rule, then we must repeat that action, until we get it right, so to speak - this is karma.

Think of karma as more like opportunities for us. We must fulfill our opportunities given to us, by us, to attain our highest levels toward our karmic state of well-doing, as well as well-being. Karma also applies to everything we do, including addictions, or excesses, of indulgences which we may have with the physical world.

Look at karma as a gift to us, by and through us. We are so far removed from the one source, that we must remember our origins and seek them out in order to return to God or our source. Karma enables us to remember and progress further in our spiritual awakening. Remember it can take time to shed your karma, but you are responsible for yourself and your actions. Your actions got you here. This cannot be denied.

The golden rules, applies: Judge others and you will be judged – Know thyself and you will come to know God, and treat others as you would like to be treated.

In a lot of cases, karmic debt isn't so easily erased. I myself have released a lot of my bigger debts, through my other lifetimes, to get to where I am today. So I discovered my karmic debts in this life were overall, fairly small. With continued use of understanding and experience, your knowledge will continue to increase. Without putting your new understandings into use, you can lose or forget your new acquired knowledge. So you must put your new knowledge into use. It took me years to erase only a few debts. Then the frequency of my karmic debts increased to every few months, then to a month, then weeks.

In the present, I already know when karma is coming my way because of my actions, I can feel and see the energy patterns already forming in the surrounding air, so to speak. The debt being created to experience it and I usually experience the debt within a few days or few hours now, instead of months, years and future lifetimes. So I am always very mindful of my own actions.

My life experience is for you, the reader, to see firsthand, what you are capable of, and what you might experience, if you decide to proceed with oneness as part of your own life. As you advance in oneness you will come to find that your suffering is to help others. At this point, just like Jesus and many others, you could easily force your surroundings around you to stop others from hurting you. However, through understanding you realize that you would only be hurting your fellow man if you stopped them from hurting you. The same applies to publicly showing certain abilities, so to speak, such as water to wine.

Now you're probably thinking to yourself, how do I know if it's my own karmic debt, or the karmic debt of others? At first, as you are releasing your karmic debts, and it can be very difficult to see and feel the difference, between your own karmic debts and other's karmic debts. But, as you are closer to ending some of your debts, you will feel yourself becoming freer, lighter and calmer about all situations you are in and around.

You also begin to understand the difference between your own debts, and other debts, brought on to you from others. For example, you can feel your own debts weighing you down, and holding you down from within. Karmic debts from others, you will come to understand and feel, as if they are external to you. More of a push and/or pull feeling on you versus a weight. As, time goes on and your understanding increases, and your own personal debts decrease, you will come to see and feel other's debts coming to you, before they hit as a surprise to you, as they will come as a surprise to most that choose not to practice oneness. A lot of people like the drama of life, their preoccupation with drama. That preoccupation with drama lets them ignore their own problems that they need to deal with.

. With most of those who are close to me, I can generally tell those around me days to months ahead of things and/or situations that are coming to them personally. I don't outright tell them specifically, the exactness of what is coming. I only start to give hints that we should start to prepare for this or that. Sometimes they heed my warnings, and when it comes to be….it's not as bad. Other times, the information given seems to be intentionally ignored, and then it hits. If I say exactly the events and/or situations coming to them, I could change their own growth. So a hint or choice is given to them for them to decide and think on. If I change things myself, I change their course of awakening.

So always be mindful of all of your actions taken towards others and yourself. Treat everybody equally and always try to help others even in your thoughts. All thoughts and actions towards others and yourself are judged to the three golden rules.

Oneness

Everybody always wants to know their future, especially day by day, and even hour by hour. I can help with this. It's exciting at first, but then it loses its appeal very fast. Nothing becomes a surprise to you. Sometimes, especially at first, you try to intentionally change things and/or situations. Sometimes they will change by themselves, and sometimes they won't.

With progressive understanding, you come to realize that you should only attempt to change the little things consciously, because of karma and natural spiritual law. I'm at a point in my life, and have been since I was thirty-two to consciously, at will, just bypass my conscious mind, and bring my soul out to the forefront of my being. So I rarely meditate anymore, because I'm generally always calm, and can achieve oneness almost instantly, if I choose.

Calmness is a key to oneness. They assist each other. Just know that everything has it's time, and it's purpose, and it all works out. I can't stress enough that everything works out exactly as it should. Keep in mind, that there is nothing in this world of physicality to even stress or worry about. Your here in physicality so enjoy it!

I can choose to leave my body, at will, anytime. Sometimes, I will still get angry over something completely stupid and petty (Usually with electronics), just to feel the emotion of being angry or frustrated and keeping myself, grounded. I do this because it can be very frustrating understanding most of the things that go on around you, the world and others, and a lot of the time, I have to take a back seat, so to speak, and just let it happen for the betterment of all involved.

I would say frustration is my biggest emotion that I might show. I'm also saddened by how the world overall treats each other. Such a huge disappointment to watch and feel. How little we have gained over time.

If you're going to let oneness become a big part of your life, I'm simply giving you the information in reference to what will come from it. A good part of my life, I can appear to be emotionless and happy because of the understandings I have, except when I can see the good deeds done for others. Generally, I just try to put others at ease, and just laugh at life. Laughter is so very good for you. Just remember the Golden Rule----you are here to help your brethren in whatever means that they feel they must do, or play out. Treat others as you would like to be treated yourself. It's all about spiritual awakening for everybody, not just for yourself.

Oneness obviously is a very big part of my life, so let's continue on with it. Through oneness I have experienced so much. To give you some examples, I can feel what the Earth feels. I can feel upcoming problems within society, and I can influence weather patterns to a degree, because weather does have its patterns created to follow from our own energies of society, but you can influence or move weather around intentionally for a short time 30 min max. It still has its pattern of flow to its destination that it must complete. I can experience any and all psychic abilities known, and yet to be discovered, and I can tune into anybody's mind or thoughts (though generally those around me, most of the time, I block intentionally). I can leave my body and travel anywhere, almost anytime I choose and I can very easily transition over to the fourth dimension----which I will talk a lot about later on. I can "See," the energy patterns flowing in everything around me-----whether it's a chair, flower, tree, air, pets, rock, the Earth and on up to our own energy patterns flowing throughout our bodies.

I can prolong passing on for others, healing of anything----plants, trees, pets, and our own bodies. I can tell you about almost anything of another person, living or not, and a lot more things. Through oneness, anything imagined, and anything to be imagined, is possible. It is the key, but you must come to use it, to understand yourself, and help others. If you don't, and try to use it for other motivations, that little immutable law of karmic debt will hit you, and probably very fast, in regards to your oneness. Any motive outside of what I have mentioned is not worth the cost of karmic debt.

With patience and increased understanding, you will come to know this, and why. Just as every day of my life, I exhibit a lot of my abilities, and most people don't even realize it. There is definitely no good reason to show it to a wide-open audience, with something as lifting a chair up in mid-air, or changing the form of something. In oneness, there is no need to show physical proof of what you can do. You're only changing an illusion.

If people were simply just a little bit more aware of themselves and their surroundings every day, then they could witness what I do daily, and what others do every day. Almost every day that goes by I debate on showing what we are capable of, but doing it completely in the open in front of everybody and in front of the camera's to help people in the world to realize what we are truly capable of and gain faith in themselves, again. As I mentioned above, I show and use my abilities every day. Most just don't realize it. They are too occupied with life and preoccupation to really see the world and their surroundings for what it really is. People miss so many details in life that I can change and alter on a daily basis. Or if they almost catch it, they pretend its luck, or its a good day for them, feeling better, in less pain and etc.

Take for example, mind reading. Every conversation I have with others I already know where they are heading in the conversation right from the beginning and usually interrupt to soon. One of my flaws I show a lot. It's a big hint I do so much that others are missing. It annoys my wife and so I try to let her have her say and then respond as anybody else would afterwards like a normal conversation. Or I can ask anybody or even my wife a question that I'm trying to figure out. I'll ask it or half ask it and then boom - I say I got it. Thank you and they are just looking at me like okay? I influence a lot of things with pyscho-kinesis because it is so natural for me to use in so many ways, but most miss it and think it was more of a coincidence or luck.

Please don't believe, in the misconception, that you have to be broke, homeless, and travel around the world spreading the Word of God. There are much more effective methods, than in doing things like that. When you are in oneness you don't have any need for anything literally. You don't need to eat food or drink anything because you are getting energy from your surroundings. You don't go to the bathroom and weather won't effect you because you are blending into everything. If you're in an intermediate state let's call it - a state between oneness and trying to live that way. You will be provided for. Other's will give you food and drink when you need it. They will give you shelter if you need it. Whatever is needed will be provided.

Now I'm not just saying the above you will be provided for as a saying. My entire life has run this way for me. Anytime, in my life that I have truly needed something it has always been provided to me and a lot throughout my life. Most of my life, in fact. Whether it is money or opportunities that come up and solve the problem for me. Or I took a job because I felt propelled to take it then find out later on it came to me at the right time before I needed to use it for other things that I hadn't even planned on, but came about afterwards. There is just so many different ways it has helped me in one way or another. So that's why I live my life really without worry, because I know I will always be provided for if I truly need something.

It does suck in one aspect, because if I really want something, but I don't truly need it, then it won't happen no matter what I throw at it or try to achieve to get it. Just won't happen. Or if it does happen, I will eventually have to sell it or get rid of it down the road to fulfill another need that would arise in the future.

First, let's look at yourself, and see what and who you can help around you, and it doesn't have to be with money. For example, I see lots of different people every day, be it through the work I do, through meetings, and/or in restaurants, or even the car next to me. Since I am generally aware of what is going on in people's lives, I talk to them subconsciously, or even consciously. I send out energy to help them with their problems, or what they consider to be problems, and/or good comforting thoughts to them, to make them feel reassured about their situations, and that it is going to all work out!

When I want to reach out to somebody in conversation, we will be talking about whatever, and I can throw in a weird sentence, or a few key words to them. Most over look it, and continue on with the conversation, but in that one sentence or words, that I have specifically chosen, I am reaching out directly into their subconscious. You're subconscious remembers and records all on a vibrational wave. Through the subconscious, the energy or words with energy go directly to their soul, and helps them out or gives them something for them to think about or replay in their mind.

The conscious mind can be bypassed very easily. The only focus, and job of the conscious mind, is for its third dimensional senses, and that's all.

Anytime during the day, I can reach out to several people at once, and help them. When I sleep, I have reached over twenty five people, at a time. Here is a hint: Say, you're doing your daily routine of whatever, the routine is mindless to you, and then, "pop," all of a sudden you see your spouse, child, neighbor, boss, or co-worker, in your head. It feels, to you, like it's out of nowhere and just a simple thought you got, but that person or persons are thinking or talking about you in that exact moment, and whether it is good or bad, you can see and feel it.

Like the internet with email. At that moment, you can tap into their thoughts and/or subconscious, and ask them questions. When a person thinks about another person their energy or a vibrational link goes out to that person they are talking with and/or about and it can be felt by that other person. When you feel this person's image, "pop," into your head. You can "ride," the "vibrational link," back to them. They have opened the door to you, and you can walk back through it, to get to them. Not physically, but mentally (telepathy). Do you see? This is how one can help an unlimited number of people with energy. Through the vibrational link, that is how one can communicate with lots of people at one moment in time and space.

One nice thing with oneness too, is when people try to trick, lie, or use you, in some way; generally, karma comes back to them within hours to days. You can just see it starting to form around them. I have intentionally let it happen to me to help them (I realize this may sound difficult), but remember, they believe this is what they need, so let them do it unto me. Then I have heard of karma hitting them back, within hours, days to weeks later, in bringing them trouble, with what they had caused or were doing. That is one beauty of oneness. Everything you create around yourself and everything that is brought onto you from others, acts very quickly to you and/or the other individuals with karma.

Oneness should only be desired, if you want to bring about your own spiritual awakening. If this is what you desire, then oneness is absolutely the key. It opens all doors. Physically and mentally, the more you use oneness and/or live in oneness, the more your physical and mental body will be transformed. You won't turn into something else, but your physical and mental body, will become more aligned, tuned and in balance with vibrations.

You see, when your bodies become aligned, they become aligned down past the atomic level of your being, to the vibrational forces or waves. Trust me, I can eat or drink or do anything I want to do without effect on my body. I'm not saying that you should do any of this; it's just an example of the possibility. If I chose another path for myself then I will already realize that I will have some consequences to deal with like most do. Our bodies are amazing structures, but they need your soul's nourishment that has the vibrational wave that balances it all.

In my family, my children and wife, when they get sick with flu, virus or whatever, it's a habit in my family(used too - then they got older), which they will lay next to me at night. Sometimes, I will heal them during the day, and sometimes I will refuse for their own awakening. But, if they cuddle up to me at night, and they can stay cuddled up to me for even just a short while, and take the intense heat that I give off naturally, with my own healing, they will generally be healed in the morning, or at least be a lot better off.

In oneness, your body will change, big time, in your glandular systems, and throughout every atom and vibrational force within your body. Your glands are extremely important in your body. It's your direct physical-to-soul connections, next to your nerves. Our bodies are made of pure energy, not physical. Physical is the effect. The illusion is that everything around you is solid and real.

Think of your body as a rechargeable battery, it actually is. You sleep to recharge. All life forms need to sleep to recharge, at least in the physical or third dimension. Your soul is of pure energy that charges you up. Your glands are your batteries. So increased awakening will only benefit you substantially.

Your soul can keep you energized, as long as you need it to, if your motives are pure and not greedy. Greed causes many problems, including, the fear that you must accumulate, to be successful. Remember, moments not quantity of material. Material is non-existent. Moments are forever - literally encoded down to the DNA, cells and future's to come as they are passed on.

I am also against blood transfusions in some ways. Yes, they help a lot of people and that is a good thing. More studies should be completed on this, to include organ transplants. Scientists must study each individual down to their beliefs and awareness. People make changes to their DNA, atomic and vibrational forces, as far as, how they choose to live their lives. All the cells of your body have memories.

When blood and organs are transferred, those memories in the cells of others do transfer over. This is where rejection can occur outside the obvious scientific reasons. For example, if you would take some of my blood and transfer it to somebody else, it could have traumatic results to that individual. My blood will try to transform the rest of the host's body fluids, to change and increase, its vibrational level. Their fluids will change which will cause further changes in their glandular health, and so on, which will cause psychological changes, as well. Or their body will reject its vibrations, and will cause lots of physical problems, in trying to combat it. I am for it, when it is needed. Hint to scientists: You can create a man made neutral blood type plasma to use over blood and you can also change red blood types on any person or organ. You just have to push or pull out the blood the re-insert with new blood type. Organs are neutral to blood types.

Remember in these cases, whether its organ or blood transfusions you must change what you are doing, or it will occur again, or in a similar manner. These are given to you as a temporary solution to learn from. Just like cancer and many other diseases. You might stop it temporarily, but if the causes of it aren't fixed then it will come back even more aggressive than it was before. Why, because you bought yourself time to learn why and make the appropriate changes. If you do, then like karma grace will come in and it is gone for good. If not, then the time you bought yourself must be brought back at a faster pace to equal the time line you were heading in in the first place.

My final thoughts on oneness: As oneness is achieved almost daily, you will feel and see that you live in two worlds. One is physical with a body, senses and an ego. The second world encompasses the physical realm, and sees that you can blend into either world at any time. You truly see the physical realm as simply one big played out illusion, movie or play with unlimited mini-series's happening everywhere. It is only created vibrations that the physical body can experience and thus we can feel, see, and hear the physical vibrations through a body. In the second world, you can see all of the energy patterns of vibrations, of the physical world swirling and mixing together as a whole in the macro view and the separate in the micro view all producing movement forward thus creating obvious patterns of what is to become (the future). So if you want to know the your future or anyone else's hit oneness or even touch upon oneness and you will start to see the patterns in motion creating the futures to be.

In oneness you realize you can transcend into either realm, and experience both realms at the same time, if you choose. Now the beauty of oneness is pure freedom of all attachments and forms. Your ego still can desire what it enjoys, but the attachment to it is void. You realize that, at will, you could simply satisfy all of your ego's desires through simple thought, thus this thought creates the ego to become detached from your physical body. Ego is a built in survival mode of the physical body. It was created so we may become a part of the physical world, and be able to experience it with all of our senses and drives of the body. That is the ego's job - self protection or at least, what you consider you need protected.

In oneness you have no fears of death or of any obstacle or surroundings, because you can transcend into any form you choose. So the passing of a physical body is nothing. If your family and the world was more aware, they would realize that they could communicate with you as if you were still around with a physical body. Hint: As a society as a whole, is simply only one step away from this awareness. That vibrational link.

In oneness you truly can see the beauty of nature and everybody around you. Everything is perfect and in true harmony and motion. One of the best examples I could give you in how to live the way, or in how your life can be lived out, is through the observation of nature.

Nature shows us the way in how to live, within a physical realm. Nature grows, endures, spreads to others, dies and lives again. I like to use trees as examples of how life should be lived. Trees are very calming to me as nature is to most people. Remember, nature and animals, is what attracted us in the first place to become one with the physical realm. In meditation, nature calms us because we intuitively know this is how we should live our lives, as nature does in the physical realm.

The wind blows through the trees. Some days it is calm, other days it can almost rip and tear the tree down. The tree doesn't judge, it goes on and strives to grow stronger for the next wind. Thus the wind (or life's obstacles and struggles) will make the tree strive to be stronger. In life you can flow with the wind and become stronger (spiritually) or give in to the wind, struggle, complain and eventually the wind will tear you down.

It's all natural, let life happen without judgments, and just enjoy everything around you. It is here for your pleasure and enjoyment. Or just let life tear you down, until you just give up, and wither away. The strong trees have to be ripped up from its roots to die. But even in death, the tree has left its mark in the gaping hole in the earth and the seeds of other trees it has left behind. It has truly lived.

Some days the wind is calm and relaxing to the tree. But, if the tree gets no wind or turbulence ever, the tree becomes weak, and thus can easily be knocked down. So realize all situations, whether it is economic, relationships, or your surroundings as opportunities to make you, and the others around you stronger. But, don't judge those opportunities. Take the best of each, and just flow with the wind.

If you judge those opportunities given to you, you will become stiff and brittle. Thus you can break or get sick very easily and your body starts to break down from stress. So enjoy life, every moment of life. Every moment of everything is a blessing. You might not see the reason behind the situation, but it is all for your good. Don't judge, plan, or dwell on your past. Just live life. Life is progressively forward, not the past.

Trees don't plan their lives surroundings. They simply just try to grow stronger, and live every moment, no matter what life, or nature throws their way. They only take the best of their situation and continue on.

Trees don't dwell on their pasts. It's their nature to move on and spread their seeds upon the earth to produce more of them. They are continually driven forward, never seeking their past, or trying to know their future outcome. This is living, in the way.

What I find ironic and have for decades: Why is everybody fascinated with super hero's and all of those abilities? Because everybody deep down in their soul realizes our own potential can be. It's like a calling for us. We can be like that. Just like Star Wars - you can see the future potential in that so it attracts us deep down.

If you want to know and experience, Christ Consciousness – then know and become one with complete Oneness. Complete Oneness is Christ Consciousness!!!

Ghosts and the Fourth Dimension

Let's talk about ghosts, spirits, and the fourth dimension (the spirit world), as we call it, presently. The fourth dimension, as science has called it is simply, one level higher, than that of the physical (the third dimension). The fourth dimension is not based on physical senses. In oneness, you are able to transition into the fourth dimension with ease, and eventually, by choice.

When you're in oneness, your vibrational levels change, and you become closer in line to that of the fourth dimension and its vibration. You see everything we do and everything that is given off has a particular vibration and energy. That is why people are so attracted to music. Music is one of the primary building blocks of vibration. Can get right down to your soul. so to speak. Motivate you, drive you or enlighten you. You see, all atoms of the physical world, give off, a vibration. Vibration is simply, a movement of progression, which starts the production of the physical. Vibrations exist in every dimension, and are everywhere – present. In all dimensions, the vibrations, magnetism, and gravity are the building blocks of the dimensions. In the physical, which is the effect, it is through the movement of the atoms that the physical is caused through progression (movement); thus, evolution and creation.

I am always amused about these ghost's shows that have become so popular now, traveling to all of these supposedly haunted places. Ghosts, or more appropriately worded, souls (which they are) instead of being called ghosts. They are souls that are everywhere, all of the time. Just like us day and night. It doesn't have to be night time, to see, hear, contact, or smell them. All of my life, I have been around them, as has everybody else in our society, too. Night time simply raises your other physical senses, because of your lack of sight, which makes your other senses more sensitive to everything else around you.

The fourth dimension, actually houses most of these souls who have passed-on, from their physical bodies. They can stay in the fourth dimension, or move onto other dimensions. The fourth dimension is actually bigger than our own physical three dimensional world and of all its galaxies and etc. The fourth dimension actually encapsulates the third dimension.

Think of a water globe. The container of the globe would be the fourth dimension, and everything inside the globe, would be the third dimension, except for the space in-between everything. That is where the 3rd and 4th dimension can blend together in synchrony. That energy is more important than atoms themselves. The black empty space holds and records everything in every dimension. Hint to science: If you want to discover unbelievable and unlimited energy, study and observe this area of dark energy and dark matter.

When ghost hunters (as they call themselves) are trying to locate ghosts (as they call them in haunted places), they are simply finding the souls who have not realized that their physical body has passed-on, or refuse to accept that they have passed-on (Remember, the mind is the physical creator). So these souls are simply re-living their surroundings, over and over again. They can even re-live going to the restroom, eating, cooking, getting sick, etc. Since they have experienced the third dimension, they have memories of all emotions and feelings and still believing, it is real to them.

If people only realized that there are ghosts everywhere, and not in just supposedly, haunted places. You can communicate with souls anytime and anywhere; some people try to physically talk to them. For example, even if a soul keeps re-living their world, they can still recognize and see that we are there. The difference is that they just see you, as a curiosity, in just being there and why are you in my space? As we feel them, they feel us exactly the same. Some of them can see us, as some of us can see them. This sight is not physical sight, per say.

When a soul with a physical body, or without a physical body, is looking through one's physical or subconscious eyes, the image is imprinted into the subconscious of the soul. Thus, they see the other soul, even if it is only in glimpses. They sense you as you sense them. They don't have physical eyes, just vibrations and images to go by. Most of those living in their world, just sense you, and then just ignore you as we do them. They may realize that you're there, and be asking themselves, why have you come into their world, and who are you? So they will watch and follow you in curiosity. Some can sense you can feel them or communicate with them. Some may follow you for that reason to try to reach out to you.

So for you ghost hunters out there, change your equipment to gauge or check vibrations, if you want to actually find evidence of souls that have passed-on. Yes, their energy comes off as cold spots, noises and even smells, which, is just simply a higher concentration of vibrations. It could be a soul, or just a residue of energy. The vibrations could come off as vague physical form or very simple like the true shape of our soul - an orb of light.

Everything we do in action and thought leaves a residue of vibrational energy that sits in between the atoms in the black space. That is the recorded information. The black space or dark energy is a direct contact to the fourth dimension, through the third dimension. So be nice to those souls, as you should be, to others in the physical world.

I have traveled all over the fourth dimension, when I am conscious and unconscious. Physically I don't travel there, but I can tune in almost instantly, simply by thinking about a person. I figure nearly a quarter of my life; I have been in the fourth dimension, while I have had a physical body. Sometimes, I have to be careful not to raise my vibrations too high, or my body will start to blend into the fourth dimension.

Never worry about passing-on or dying. Your friends and past relatives will be there and to help you, and encourage you. Why worry? Trust me. There is nothing to worry about, as you leave this life. You see, most of us, when we die, it is a shock, at first, which is to be expected. And yet, when others are there to help us it is much easier. So, for those of you, who worry, that you will never see your physical family, or loved one's again, I am here to say – you will, and we all do, eventually. So, in addition to "not worrying" – know this. Through oneness, you can communicate with your family and loved ones, anytime you need to. Not when you feel you need to, but when you really need it. I'm hoping as I write this – you will remember, we are all connected together.

In the fourth dimension, is where we go when we pass-on. From here, we decide what and where to go from there. It's like a bus or airport terminal. We review the experiences we had on the physical realm, decide if our actions were appropriate for our own spiritual growth, and decide what we would like to do next. We can decide to come back to physicality to learn more, or move on, to other dimensions or worlds. In general there is usually a 3 day holding pattern in the fourth dimension.

Our current karmic debt is why our population continues to grow, all based on fear re-living our same old patterns. Have you heard of the saying, history repeats itself? It does until consciousness changes.

When our bodies have passed-on, some of us don't even realize that we have expired. We continue to live our life as we know it. Incredible, but true. Say you're in the hospitable and haven't even realized you have passed on yet. You just keep re-imaging that your still there.

Our mind is our builder, and every detail we have once known on Earth, we can duplicate simply from our memory and including all of its detail. Remember, our subconscious mind remembers everything, in every detail. So when we pass-on our conscious mind passes-on, and our subconscious mind becomes our conscious mind, in the fourth and other dimensions.

So the soul continues on, until one day it realizes that something is different or family and/or friends come by, and give him/her hints, that we have relinquished our physical body. Then a light appears to us that attracts and guides us from there. A perfect explanation of what the fourth dimension is like, when we pass-on, is in the movie "The Lovely Bones". It was a movie that my oldest daughter wanted me to watch with her.

Once we move beyond the light, I'm not sure where or what happens to us. I know it's not heaven, or hell, as most of us envision it. Neither actually exists as most think of them. If you believe in hell, and think you are going to hell, then you will create a hell for yourself, to experience in the fourth dimension. If you believe you're going to heaven, then you will create a heaven for yourself, until help arrives, and the light appears. From what I can tell, the light simply moves you into a higher vibration, or resonance field, of elevated dimensions. Then one can come back to physicality or move on to other dimensions.

Not everybody is given the light, I'm sorry to have to reveal. Only when you truly come to understand and accept that you have passed on your physical body, will then the light appear for you. One can turn away from the light and stay in the fourth dimension, if they choose. When they are ready, the light will appear again for them. The light never judges and time is as long as needed for the soul. Usually these are the souls or ghosts that ghost hunters find and try to document.

So the fourth dimension is full of souls just like those on Earth. Most replaying what they choose to play out and experience. Relatives and ghost hunters can attract or pull those souls they believe, or remember, in thought, back to the third dimension of vibrations. Not in the physical sense, but just in the vibrational sense. Remember, that vibrational link of thought between each other.

Some, like me, are very sensitive to those vibrations; others are not as sensitive to them. But, anybody can become sensitive to them. It's like a fine piece of electricity or fiber optics; it's simply a natural effect of vibration and movement. In the fourth dimension, there is no sleep because sleep is only needed in the third dimension – the physical to maintain energy.

Through oneness you can become aware of souls around you, because the vibrations are so close to being the same. The vibrations that they give off and/or create are very similar to that of electricity. That's why science has found out that electronics and anything magnetic and electrical can become easily disturbed and attracted in other directions. It's simply the same energy patterns starting to attract, and repel each other.

I have problems with electronics during those times when my energy is too high. I can spend hours a day trying to use the internet and other various electronic items every day. It's very frustrating. Sometimes, my wife and kids will even ask me to leave, and go to another room, until my wife or kids can get they're homework done or watch a movie. I can also send static shocks to others several inches away from me, if my energy is too high. I interfere with the television channels quite often as I pass by electronics. Sometimes, I can dim or brighten light bulbs. Drain batteries or boost batteries. In oneness, electricity of any sort becomes attracted to you. I'm always mindful of lighting.

In the third dimension, our physical world, you don't have to mourn very long, for loved ones, who have passed-on. Let them go. The past is the past. You have the precious memories of them. Every time you think about them you can draw them back with your thoughts, or by talking about them. Remember, that vibrational link? It also connects with memories of others. This is also why there is generally a waiting period in the fourth dimension. They are giving you time to mourn and understand. It also gives passed on souls the opportunity to come to the realization that they no longer have a physical body.

Since the third and fourth dimensions are so closely intertwined, one can be called back to you very quickly. When one has moved on, and/or past the fourth dimension, or even reincarnated, they can still be called back, if they choose to make the contact. Yes, even in reincarnation. Just because you have a new body doesn't mean that your soul has forgotten. Have you ever had the feeling of knowing another person, but you can't remember from where? You may see someone you feel you have known, and you feel like you know things about them, and yet don't exactly know why? You may have had a very close experiences or relationship, in a past life with them.

So let those who have passed-on, go in peace. They are perfectly fine, and in a place where physical things are not felt, and all is embraced, as always in any dimension. I suggest the best thing you can give a person who has passed-on, is good positive thoughts. For example, you have passed-on and follow the light. You love them too, so forgive them. Understand that they have done the best that they could for you with their understandings.

Forgiveness of them is the best way to release them and help them then follow and achieve what they must complete in the fourth dimension. Pray for them and give them your blessings. They will hear what you say. It's all in the vibrations.

Remember, anytime you better yourself, or hinder yourself, as in abilities, your karma will follow you everywhere. So be mindful of your thoughts – as you should towards all, even those who have done you wrong. Understand wrong-doing is only thought of; as such, through your own perception of it. To make it easier for you, think of wrong-doing, first, with the understanding of why they did something, then forgiveness can come easier. Forgiveness is a <u>must.</u> If not, then the same situation will repeat itself over and over, until you learn to forgive.

In the fourth dimension, when souls have realized they have passed-out of their physical body, they don't feel any physical pain or mental anguish, or anything negative, and they now decide what they choose to do next. So, don't worry about them.

The third dimension is a slower life, so to speak, than the fourth dimension. A perfect example of the fourth dimension, (which you experience all of the time, whether you realize it or not), is in your dreams. In your dreams, what you feel and experience is up to you. Once again the book and movie "The Lovely Bones" is exactly what it is like for trapped souls, or souls who don't want to move on. The movie with Robin Williams and Chris Neilson, "What Dreams may Come," is also a good example of what the fourth dimension is, and how souls can trap themselves in their own world of guilt and Robin Williams shows what you can do with your mind in the fourth dimension. Anything you can think of, you can create instantly.

Is possession real? Can be, but only to a degree. Simply a soul trying to occupy a body as they call it. It's actually occupying another soul, not the body, per sa. It tries to encapsulate the soul. Now here is the interesting part. Religion uses crosses and fancy words to scare the unwanted soul away basically with confidence. It's really all about confidence as if you are simply facing a bully. Once the bully is faced with true confidence in yourself with your own energy towards them telling them to leave they will leave. They might put up a fancy scary ordeal over it, but that's all it is. This is what bullies do. Bullies can put on a good show and throw out big consequences to come if you resist because deep down they know you could crush them if you acted on it. They create these fronts or shows for us. If they make you scared you lose type of thing.

As I have mentioned earlier, there is a border around myself with them. This same border can be used against them with anybody. That's why they can go crazy the closer you get to them. They can feel it. They know it can push them away from the encapsulated soul while the regular soul is unaffected by the border. Just a childish game by some that have figured out how to control another soul. It's not true control, just temporary. Does it happen a lot. Not from what I have seen. Most people deep down are very good people once you get past all the bs. So it's just the younger more messed up one's let's call them.

The Third Dimension

The third dimension was actually created through all of us with God, from the fourth dimension. It was another expression of our experiences. The physical gives us more time to experience, through patience, to help us unfold and remember our roots, if we chose too.

In the fourth dimension, remember mind is the physical creator, so everything you think, you are already experiencing instantly. In the third dimension, everything is slowed down to be able to view our results slower with atoms. It gives us more time to figure our situations out. Think of the third dimension as an active laboratory, as it has been termed. It's not really a laboratory, but think of the third dimension as simply another dimension of experience for us. Just as when we pass on our physical bodies, we move into another realm of experiences, which we can grow or hinder ourselves spiritually. The third dimension was never actually meant to be made, not for us; it was simply an extension of our own creation of neutral energy, to observe its interactions.

However, we liked our own creations so much that we desired to feel what it felt like. You see, we created it, but we didn't have the physical senses to actually experience it. So we desired to like it so much, we started to emerge ourselves into physical substance. Not like possessions of, but our separate creations of. We did emerge ourselves into trees, rocks and animals, but the experience was lacking to understand free will and desire.

As time continued on, the bodies we had created trying to duplicate nature weren't hurt and non-productive, in so far, as reproduction. We couldn't experience sex, as we saw all around us with animals, because we didn't have the primitive drive of survival. So, we created bodies that were more male and female. Thus, a single image or body was formed, to experience reproduction.

This is when Eve was created as the first physical human body with a single reproduction organ. The Bible says man came first, but it was woman who was first. Through a woman other souls could come to experience physicality. Years later Adam was created. When Adam was created (several Adams and Eves were created and put throughout different areas of the world). A tidbit of information: Jesus was actually one of the first Adams.

From this point on, all previous forms and future form's, could then be brought through the physical forms of man and woman to experience the third dimension, for those who chose to do so, including the unusual forms already created. They could pass on, and then experience, the third dimension through man's body through birth. Then, starting over, and experiencing life in one same body type, was created. One, in which, we could experience the physical with our senses, and enjoy reproduction.

Through reproduction, we were given the ability to experience the third dimension in all aspects of. Ever since, all man/woman were brought through the physical to experience the physical with senses. No more immaculate conception is possible, I'm sorry. One can blend into the third dimension from the fourth dimension, but will lack the ability to experience the physical world with its physical senses. One could pass on the physical body and then come back in form, which appears to be as real as the physical body, but would still lack the emotional senses.

Why do you think reproduction is such a big part of us, and we are the only species that enjoys reproduction supposedly? I personally, think a lot of animal species enjoy it too. It's not just a primitive response to us – it's also an experience of expression and desire for us. As time went by, our bodies have changed and evolved, to the point where we are, today. We have less hair than our predecessors, and are more erect, and have a much smaller physique. We have grown from an animal type of body, to a supposedly well mannered, separate species now. Don't get this wrong, we have never evolved from the animal species or monkeys. Yes, physical forms like the monkey, but not from the animal species. We created all of this together, do you not think we couldn't just pick a form that is versatile and simply change some of the DNA for our own to be able to think. Science will never find the jump or leap from animal to human - close to form, but not the jump. Some people can still feel, and remember, they're connection to God, have tried to help others remember who they truly were.

Religion was created a long time afterwards, to attempt to help man, remember his origins. But many things were left out of religion, as it evolved (censored). As time went by, science was created to try to help explain what religion could not; hence, their current incompatibilities. Eventually, the two will merge and come to the same conclusions in the future. The physical world is an illusion of vibrational forces. Our religion, as we know it now, will expire before science does. The future of religion will depend on what they choose to do. Not set in stone yet, so to speak, but definitely heading that way.

So from the third dimension origins, let's transcend into a combination of the physical world and the fourth dimension, as one. Let's move onto dreams.

Dreams

Your dreams, if you can remember them, are in the fourth dimension, but the senses of the dreams are connected to your physical body. When your physical body and consciousness has been laid aside, temporarily in your dreams, your subconscious mind and soul become released. Your subconscious mind first repeats the events of your day, like a tape recorder. Your subconscious mind reviews what changes it should, or should have not have done, during the day based on your souls ideals. Your subconscious reviews the day in reverse starting from your last thought and action before you went to sleep, to when you awake in the morning.

During the process your soul is cruising around in the fourth dimension, doing its thing, talking to other souls and absorbing energy. Your soul needs very little time to absorb plenty of energy for itself. Your soul comes back to your body and reviews the information with suggestions. This process can take less than a second to do, and only minutes for the information to be absorbed into the mind. The more you play in drama of life, push your physical body hard and mentally exhaust yourself, the more energy your soul needs to absorb, which means you will want to more sleep. Like draining a battery down with harder use.

All animals with a brain or no brain, dream. But, they dream of being awake because they can't comprehend they're being in creation or any other way. Their bodies need to rest, too, through neutral energy while their brains continue to operate as ours do. They dream as if they were still awake and active. This is why they can sleep a lot of hours during the day, because they still feel that they are awake and active. They are like batteries too. They too need to rest and absorb energy.

You have three different or types of dreams each night. The first is when the soul comes back and reviews suggestions with your mind, which you rarely remember. The second dream you have would be what the outcomes of your decisions have been created for you, in the next day, or future events to come. This is more like a repeating dream or theme that keeps coming up here and there. The third dream, which is the one most people remember, if they remember their dreams at all, are suggestions of what to do, coincidences to come, including physical happenings, wishes you desire, a review back to the mind of what they should have done, throughout the day, there own moral, so to speak.

The third dream always lasts the longest. It's almost equal to two thirds of your dream-state. It's the one that is trying to give you clues as to what is to come, and how you should react to such situations. It's the part you should try to remember. This third part of dreams is generally broken-up with several mini dreams or soap operas of any and all subjects desired. Some have a few, while most I have observed, have almost a dozen or more – like a mini-series, but each with its own scenarios. The dreams you remember the most, are the ones that you have repeated several times in your dream state. Your soul and subconscious are really trying to imprint these dreams to you to remember in your waking state.

While in your dream state or I prefer consciously awake, you can tap into other people's dreams. I figured since I could tap into other's thoughts, maybe I could tap into their thoughts when they were dreaming. I was curious what my children were seeing in their dreams, when they were having nightmares. So I tried it, and it worked.

So then, I tried it on lots of individuals, to get it down. I do it while I am conscious so I can control my movements. Over time, I learned how to tap into others dream state when I was in my own dream state. But, my dream state I am in complete control whenever I chose to be.

You can always check yourself with another to see if you have really tapped into their dream. Ask a friend when they wake up, if they saw you in their dream, if they remember their dreams.

You see, through imagery you can project your essence (vibrational state) into another's dream state like trans-meditation. I do it at will within minutes or during my dream state at various times when others call on me. But, I would recommend using it through meditation first. When you have relaxed your body and mind, then from here, as I have mentioned in my meditation chapter, you visualize the person's face and head you would like to tap into. I would imagine them for a couple of minutes, until you get this part of the process down. From here, then visualize your body energy wave or soul leaving your body and going into their head. Keep projecting this, until you can see the clouds or a thick haze. If you see the clouds, you're in. Then get used to traveling as if you were floating or flying. from above. Your head becomes your movement of where you want to go or fly to. Your body simply follows your heads movement.

I've never really taught anybody how to do this, except in this manner with dreams. So it will probably take several times or more to get this down. I would also recommend improvising the methods I gave you that may be easier for you to try to tap into. I don't know of any books out there on tapping into other's dreams, to help you out. But, I found it quite easy for me to do, probably because I can so easily tap into others thoughts.

When you tap in, most individuals will remember you having been in their dream, because usually when you appear in their dream, it temporarily spooks them. If something spooks or shocks them they will remember it. I like to describe dreams as watching a theater or play in motion. Dreams are isolated. Meaning they are contained within one's mind. So if you just magically walk into one of the plays that will spook them at first.

What I discovered is that when you tap into a dream, you always enter the dream from above. Meaning, when you break into a dream the first thing you will come across is clouds. Not really clouds, but they are grey, and never give you anything to see, i.e., no visibility.

You always enter into a dream as if you were flying or floating in the air through the clouds. As you descend into the clouds, eventually you will break through, and everything around you will be dark or black, as if, it was night time. You can look up and see the "clouds" that you have just descended through, and then look downwards or to the side, and see something like an open theater all lit up. This theater is their dream in motion. You can stay there in between in the darkness and just observe, or descend until you move into the "play" or dream in motion.

You will be observing the person acting-out their dream, and any characters they need to fulfill their dream. Until you enter the play, they have no idea that you are there. Once you enter into their play, they will notice you. If they know you, they will continue on with their dream pretty much ignoring you. If they don't know who you are, generally the play in motion will freeze up and stop. Once they get over you, the dream will continue on where it had left off. At this point, you can sit down and talk to them, so to speak, if this is your purpose.

I only enter into dreams with the highest intentions of helping others. From this point, I can examine problems. With my children, I discovered when they were having nightmares, what the nightmares were actually connected to, was their physical body. Their physical body was in pain, or supposed pain, or they had an upcoming cold, or virus kicking-in. The images of a scary movie can be re-created in a dream to appear real to give signals to them and the body about upcoming situations. Remember, our subconscious minds can use images that have created emotions within us to us those images to provoke a better response to us in the conscious mind because the conscious mind understands emotions. Thus, nightmares or the opposites of it.

Everybody can remember their dreams. It's simply a matter of, "wanting", to remember. If you want to remember your dreams, follow these steps and you will. Before you go to bed and fall asleep tell yourself-when I wake up, I am going to remember my dreams. Keep repeating this to yourself as your falling asleep. Put a pad of paper and pen next to your bed or night stand. When you wake up in the morning while you are still in a little daze, or a little sleepy, lay there and think back on what you dreamed. Repeat it several times before you get up. Once you get up, write your dreams down immediately. This may take several times, but this method, will work. Once your conscious mind becomes fully awake it will be harder to retrieve those images unless they are more emotional type of dreams like nightmares.

My method is a little bit different, because I can consciously remember my dreams, and even change my dreams around, if I don't like them, or replay the dreams over and over giving them different endings or change the middle of them while I dream. You can do the same with practice. Anything I can do you can do and more! So dreams to me aren't of much relevance, because I can change them at-will and do quite often several times a night. You see, as my day proceeds my soul already analyzes my daily routine throughout my day because of my calmness and oneness. So my dreams are simply, what I choose to do. Half of the time, I just let my mind dream of what it chooses, just like everybody else. Sometimes, it can be scary, but I realize I can change it if I want to or go thru the emotions of being scared or achieve something that would be impossible in the physical world to do - like flying around. When I choose to remember my dreams, I can get up in the morning, and do my thing. My conscious mind has very little influence on what I have dreamt about. I will remember my dreams for as long as I choose to, before I let them go. Sleep for myself is generally for my soul to re-energize itself.

Why would you want to remember your dreams? Because your dreams pass on all kinds of information to you…information related to the health of your physical body, mental body, spiritual well-being, and even insights into your future. Your conscious mind has difficult time translating information from your subconscious and soul into words. So a majority of your dreams will be passed on to you, through your consciousness, with symbols and images of a dream playing out like real life. The mini-series of theaters. From here, your conscious mind can see the images and/or plays and translate them into words and meanings that it has learned.

Dreams are an excellent way to get clues about the condition of your physical body, if you haven't become sensitive to it yet through meditation. Dreams help try to warn you with upcoming patterns and situations that it can see coming your way and how you should deal and/or handle them. I have had many of these throughout my life. Now do I choose to listen to them. Sometimes and sometimes not. Dreams, just like intuition is some of the best forms of receiving information for yourself. Your answers are coming directly from your soul to yourself.

So I encourage all to take notes and remember your dreams. Say you have an invention or problem to solve in the physical. Before, you go to bed, think of this problem over and over while you're falling to sleep. In doing this your dreams will send you the answers you are looking for. It's simply a matter of your remembering. Sometimes, when you wake up it will be an inspiration to yourself. Then you have answered your question. I do this a lot. When I wake up I have so many answers to various questions that I have been trying to solve or figure out the best way to proceed in a situation. So much vital information is in your dreams for you to use in your daily living. I can even take a nap and do the same thing. I wake up and have the answers I was seeking.

For those of you, who still think that dreams are in black and white? They definitely aren't. Your dreams have every color in the physical world and more. My colors in dreams are much clearer, sharper, richer and even more colorful than I can see physically. It's really quite amazing and it is how you will experience colors when you pass on. Just so much better.

Spirits, Angels and Demons

Let's move on to, what we call spirits, angles, demons, and such. I've seen and been around a lot of things. I have not seen any so called angels with wings, demons or a devil of any kind. I'm sorry. What I have seen is, is other soul's projecting images of themselves, to the person they are trying to help, that comforts, or looks bad to them. Remember, that vibrational link that I talked about. Souls that are past the fourth dimension can tap this link much more efficiently and thus your thoughts are an open book to them. Some would call them their angels and/or guides to them.

You see, all there is, is each other, and our source, which we call God. We are all here to help each other – some do, and some choose not to. But, as souls in the fourth dimension and higher dimensions, many of billions of other souls try to help us, in the third dimension and other dimensions, in order to help their own awakening and your awakening. So projecting a comfortable image to us makes it easier, and/or more pleasing, to our own senses, so you will accept their understandings. Thus a religious person if they see an image of an angel that will be a more powerful and profound image to them.

Throughout time and various religions, it has almost always been pleasing for people to see a human body figure with wings, called angels. I thought I was seeing angels in my younger years, until I progressed enough in my knowledge and understanding, that some of my guides eventually revealed to me, who they were. Another soul, as we all are, simply trying to help me in my spiritual awakening. You see, my background originally was one of Christianity. So those projections were easier for me to accept and respond to initially as angels and such.

I, myself have been called an angel so many many many times over, by others in a physical body, as well as from others in the fourth dimension. This is their perception of me. Now some angels as others think of them can be thought of as arc angels. Really all an arc angel is an elder soul. The energy given off by them and referenced to in many minds think they are arc angels. But, really those supposed angels are simply of the eldest. Achieve oneness and you'll come to understand who and what an eldest is. There energy can pass through into the third dimension and actually effect the physical surroundings as if they have physical control in the physical but without a physical body. They are unique.

All minds are connected together, on a single vibration that extends throughout all dimensions. All you have to do is picture their image or have that individual think on your image. This is how you tap into the subconscious record of anybody, and retrieve most information about them.

Much like, all of our records today, are public information, accessible to all. Again – once more for emphasis – we are all connected, as one. We are all blown away and in awe by the beauty, mysteries and size of the universe, but if you knew that vibrational link is. It can make our entire universe seem petty and small to the all of it all and then there is more beyond even that. Our universe even unfathomably huge is just one small piece of it all.

Records of Information

You see, there are two places for records of information that you can access. The one I just gave you (the vibrational link that I keep talking about). The other one, is a place full of white light emitting out from everything, and appears to have columns, with a quiet older man, who welcomes you, while pointing to a huge book. It appears to be about two feet wide. Two and half feet tall were lying on an art board. He opens the book, or sometimes you are allowed to open the book. No words are spoken between you and the man. In the book a page is opened up and you simply read from it, and the words are big and easy to read, while the words just seem to scroll through never leaving a single page. Your imagery of this place may be different. Perhaps this is what I imagined it to look like for the comfort of myself.

I have read from Edgar Cayce's books that Edgar Cayce called this place the "Hall of Records," and this book he referred to, as "The Akashic Records". I believe it's a place where all information about everything since conception and beyond, can be found. I rarely touch this place anymore because it is a lot easier for me to just touch the vibrational wave that flows through all, to retrieve information. Now if you're channeling with your subconscious, this place would be ideal for one to tap into for information. I can see it being very efficient for the subconscious to access.

Being that I rarely use this form, I would recommend reading up on books by Edgar Cayce on self hypnosis. I'm sure he has a book on both. The name of them I don't know, since I rarely read anything on the metaphysical, spiritual and psychic abilities anymore.

Soul Helpers/Spirit Guides

Souls in other dimensions have advanced or awakened to a point where they only choose to help other souls like us, in the third, fourth, and other dimensions. You can call these souls more like spirit guides, as I have seen mentioned in books, but they are simply souls just like you and I. Their whole purpose is being driven to help us. They can stay and help one soul during all of its physical life, or they can be shared by many souls, which is more the case.

The difference between a spirit guide and an angel is that the angels are more specific and come in at very specific times to help. Stronger and more pronounced when they enter or leave. Angels can actually effect the physical surroundings around somebody as a spirit guide can not. Spirit guides literally all they do is trying to help others with their awakening. A better name for them is teachers. When a person is channeling in general this is who they are contacting is spirit guides. They come in many varieties, types and sizes, so to speak.

Most spirit guides are not around us 24/7. They have other souls to help, and their own goals to achieve as well. You can become sensitive to these souls through channeling yourself through meditation. However, you don't have to achieve meditation, to speak with your "helpers," as I prefer to call them. Some of us can communicate with their "helpers" simply by asking them questions, which generally takes time, sensitivity and practice to develop.

Some people are naturally more sensitive to vibrations that surround us all. Meaning psychics, for example, you can ask them a question, and they ask their helper or spirit guide the question. The helper then finds or locates the individual where the question is being asked. The guide then asks that soul the question. The question is generally answered and relayed back to the psychic. The psychic then relays the answer.

I actually prefer talking directly to you or into your own soul. This way the information is directly from your soul with your emotions. Achieve oneness and this method will become commonplace for you to use. I have the ability to communicate directly with your soul, no middleman. I'm not saying that the helpers would give you wrong information or elusive information, but I prefer to hear it directly from your soul unless the question is not about you. You ask a question then boom I have the info for you just like that. Now if I don't get any information, then I'm not allowed to answer your question for you whether it is from timing or your motives.

When I am looking at your soul development and needs. I care less about answering your direct questions. I want to give you a direct answer with understanding behind it. Helpers for example, can be monotone in their information, and limited to that specific question. Your soul tells me a lot more about you. I can get the answer to your question, plus at the same time, truly see what motivates you and then I can pass your conscious mind and drop words of information into your subconscious to get to your soul. This is how I can touch anybodies soul with my words.

Countless times I have learned that my words do make changes within individuals. Since then I have learned over years of practice that I can make changes to anybody spiritually, even skeptics. Sometimes, the changes can be noticed within minutes or days up to years to take effect depending upon how closed minded they are and resist what I have told them. But, my words, either written or spoken to you directly drop a little seed within your subconscious and soul that slowly starts to grow and branch out until you react to it. Thus, the warning I gave with my book. Do not read this book, if you don't want your life to change in some manner spiritually.

Most have three to four helpers that try to help give your soul suggestions throughout your Earth life. You see, time only applies to us. Time is actually all one second. A couple of times I have been granted the ability to try to experience the past, present and future in how it really is. I've only had quick one to three second bursts or glimpses. It's very hard for the conscious mind to be able to see and try to even comprehend what is going on. It becomes instantly disoriented, and you can just feel it trying to figure out what is going on and trying to organize the information. The conscious mind is trying to keep up with all of the subjects being thrown at it, practically all at the same time. I feel that I was granted the chance to see it, to provide it to others; although it came to me in glimpses only and still very difficult to try to explain to others.

The past, present, and future are re-writing themselves continually. There is no past, except on the record of time, as I call it, and the vibrational wave which can also leave some residue like our minds memories. The glimpse I saw, I saw, what I just did, the present happening now, and the future to be, happening, all at once. So sorry, but time travel is out of the question physically, but matter can intermingle when transported back. Meaning you have to change your perception of time to travel into or back into time because it's all one. Just like a vibration can move one way or the other and even in multiple directions all at once. In the physical sense of having a body it can only move forward. You can speed up or slow your movement down though or even bend it in the physical.

Now through records of time, the vibrations stay, but everything else re-writes itself over, instantly. Everything is progressive evolution, but constantly, every moment re-writes itself, kind of like tape recording over something. It's hard to explain, and probably harder for others to realize that everything physical, is constantly duplicating itself. Teleportation is possible, because it is progressively forward, and will become reality someday, just like food replication will be. Think Star Wars.

As you can become sensitive to your guides through meditation, channeling or oneness, you can talk to them directly within your mind. You can ask them a question and they will respond back with an answer.

Communication with them is very easy. Harder to get it down for the first time, but once you achieve it, it becomes easier to communicate with them the more you use it until its second nature to you. In your meditation, when you are calm and relaxed, project your questions or thoughts outward from your body. From here, clear your mind and just wait. Be patient, until all of a sudden an answer just "pops," into your head as an idea, images or words. You will recognize the difference between your own thoughts and then thoughts that just pop in there.

Now how do your guides get their information? The three methods I have talked about with the Akashic records, the vibrational link and they can draw on their own experiences, as well. I'll give you an example of how the vibrational link can happen within seconds to retrieve information. I do this when I need to help souls in the fourth dimension. But, it is the same method that our guides use with us. With our guides, it is very easy for them to tap into the "Akashic records," as Edgar Cayce calls it because they are already unconscious.

Once I hit a point of knowledge and experience I was shocked at first, when I had a passed-on soul, coming to me consciously from the fourth dimension, to ask me questions. The first time I experienced this, I was sitting on my bed going through some paperwork, when boom, out of nowhere, this soul was sitting next to me, a small 12 year old girl, and was asking me questions. At first, I had no idea about the questions she was asking me. I had no answers, and was still a little baffled about it. Why was she coming to me? I was asking myself why is a "ghost" coming to me? Why not go to another "ghost" or helper? I didn't want to tell her that I have no idea for you. I'm sorry. Then all of a sudden, all at once, I had all of the answers to her questions. They came out of nowhere from this vibrational link that connected to her.

With that same information given to me, I knew who she was, the answers to her questions, and how far she had traveled to find me, specifically. It was a good distance away in the fourth dimension, as if one traveled from Europe to California. Since then I have had many others show up, out of nowhere, asking me questions. I still get a little excited when they show up, and I always have the answers, except most of the questions they ask me now are about what I am writing to you about. They are questions I already know within, and I know how to help them progress. With this twelve year old girl soul, since I didn't want to let her down, but I had confidence in myself that I would be able to help her with her questions. My soul simply touched her vibrational link and retrieved the information for me to answer her questions. This is what your guides do for you if they can't answer the question directly with their own experiences.

Just remember, not all questions can be answered. Some questions you are not allowed to give to the person. So in my case, my mind stays blank, which tells me that I am not allowed to answer that question for them for whatever reason. I won't know why I can't give them the information either.

As long as I can remember, souls or ghosts have always been attracted to me. But, unless I gave them my approval, they would always keep about ten feet away from me. It's something my wife and my kids have come to accept, being around me because they can generally sense them around, in one way or another. Sometimes ghosts the younger and more playful move our objects around, throughout the day and night. Objects that interest them, not like car keys. They like to hide items, like our children's toys, my wife's jewelry, and my paperwork. On random occasions we will have left our items set in specific places, and then when we go to get them, they are gone. Then we'll come home, and see the items sitting right there in front of us on the kitchen table or kitchen counter in a completely obvious place where we don't put our items. Like they are kids playing hide and seek with us.

We've learned they like to return the items in places where we can't miss them, and in full plain view, with no other items around them. I quickly learned, when I was younger, that I could move towards these souls, and they would back away, or move to the side of me, but always keeping that distance, unless I gave them permission to come closer to me, and it didn't have to be spoken permission, with any words. Once I realized this, it was like having a continuous audience around you. Privacy was out the door. This was something I had to learn to accept. The exception, is when souls ghosts come to me asking me questions of me. They can get right next to me.

The souls usually just hang around and watch me. Sometimes they would hang around my residence waiting for me to come back home, or just follow me to work and that was a little bit weird. Other souls never did anything except to just hang around me, and watch me for a while and then go away. My wife and children have all had to get use to this and just accept it as I have.

I was worried, in 1998 when I was twenty seven years old, and my helpers told me that my time had come, and that I had acquired enough remembrance and experience. They told me: "Now the time has come for your choosing in this life and/or in your next life to selflessly serve, witness and sacrifice for others. From now on all answers you have will be answered through the communion of the one source which connects all. Through yourself you will have all the answers you need, and seek to help others. We can no longer serve you because now you have awakened to become one of our teachers again. Rejoice".

This was a little scary for me at first. You have to understand that I have had my guides around me for as long as I could remember, as everybody else does too. Now they are gone and all information is up to myself to gain.

From what I have observed, most helpers always stay around the soul they are helping, for most of their lives. So, why was mine leaving now, and for good? Even with them telling me this, I still had to soak it in and then accept it. Most souls, in the third dimension, have two to four helpers helping them. For me, I have always had around twelve helpers watching over me, each with their specialty of knowledge and experience. Once I maxed out their knowledge or experience another one would come in to advance upon it. I have asked about that, as well, but their answer was always the same. This is an answer we are not allowed to tell you, in time you will come to know why for the answers you already know.

Since then; However I have been, pretty much on my own, and my protection and knowledge has come from within, for my continued advancement and awakening. It's mostly just been these advanced concepts, which I have been testing and proving. When I was younger, I didn't quite get the direction I was going with my abilities and knowledge. Just as a younger person, wouldn't realize. This has been part of my waiting and accepting. Ever since that day I have never talked to another guide again as in them teaching or helping me.

Now remember, all knowledge given to you, you already know within yourself. Your soul already has all of the answers you need, require and a lot more because your soul is connected to the source and all. Your guides are simply giving you information that appears to be new to you. But, it is simply spiritual awakening, unless its information is for others. Which through oneness, you can answer within yourself and through the individual by connecting to their soul.

As far as your own physical protection, here's a big hint: Have no fear, and don't even try to protect yourself from events, and people. It will be as it should be whatever the outcome. If you are in oneness certain elements won't arise or will be taken care of for you, unless it's your time! I say this, but I also realize that those that live in the physical do need protection because of who or what they do as a living. Otherwise, emotional, greed and mentally ill people will try to get you. If they were taking more of a path of oneness, the need for protection wouldn't really be needed. I personally have been physically protected or removed from many many many situations that otherwise, I should not be here. I always thought they were from my guides, but realized later on those were angels that physically moved things around in the physical.

Your helpers change according to the change in the information you need to learn. Once they have taught you everything they can, they then leave, and someone else comes in who is more advanced or awakened in their knowledge and experience, to continue to help you in your progression. Most of us will keep the same ones throughout our whole physical life unless you are advancing fast in spirituality.

Anybody can be a guide to you living or non-living. Simply open up and let others help you in your awakening. There is as much help in the physical as there is from one's non-physical. If you're open to all of the opportunities around you every day in life you will see that you are constantly guided to meet your next opportunity or opportunities culminating to a bigger opportunity. Every day I watch the opportunities given to others and they simply ignore it and continue on with their physical motions of life. Only sometimes, when somebody looks back at their past and then puzzles the pieces together to see that each opportunity whether taken as negative or positive has taken them to the place they need to be in in the present. That is one reason of why we can remember things from our past. Open up to oneness and you will see your opportunities given to you and others all of the time. I use the word opportunities not in definition to financial gain, but as in choices given to help others and awaken yourself spiritually.

Soul Light

Let's talk, here, about the light that most souls, leaving the third dimensional world, will eventually see. I have seen it so many times over when I am moving around in the fourth dimension. The light just opens up out of nowhere for others when they are ready and have accepted that they no longer have a physical body. I have tried several times to follow the light up the tunnel, and to write about it for you, the reader. Each time it is the same – a light appearing out of nowhere in darkness. But, you can see several hundreds of tunnels opening up, looking out, throughout the fourth dimension. As you get closer to the light, you start to see a tunnel come into your sight. As you get closer to the tunnel, you will see the light coming from within the tunnel.

So, I floated over to the bottom of the tunnel which is its beginning. It looks just like a massive size tornado, but upside down, and it doesn't swirl. When you first enter the tunnel, it is dark and grayish but huge, and you can see the light still coming from the top of the tunnel. The tunnel is open at the top leading into somewhere very bright. The open tunnel of light in the top appears to be the size of a car, at first as you are looking up at it. The light is literally indescribable with words, but I will try to describe it. The light is the brightest and softest then any light you have ever seen in your life. Like looking directly into the sun, but not hurting your eyes. It's warm and extremely inviting to you, as if you just know something great is about to happen to you. So, you're propelled to follow it.

Then you are in the middle of the tunnel floating upwards to the top of the tunnel. The tunnel is dark, and as you slowly move up the tunnel following the light, the grey smooth and rough surfaces of the tunnel, the tunnel starts to get darker. About halfway up the tunnel, the walls of the tunnel start to look like there are figures and faces built into the walls, and they aren't moving. Then as you look closer at them, you can see that they are moving with the walls of the tunnel, and looking directly at you. It's weird but you feel completely safe, but you continue on because you can start to see the end of the tunnel at the top, and the light still feels so right and compelling. The beam of light is expanding in diameter as your floating upwards getting closer to the top.

As you continue on, the figures, faces and tunnel disappear. Then when you get very close to the top of the tunnel, the light is so bright and warm. You can see the top of the tunnel now. It is huge almost like seeing an open football field that is full of light coming through it. You also can see there is a room past the top of the tunnel full of light. But, here's the catch. I've tried to enter into that area several times. The first few times, I was stopped, and not allowed to enter. The last time that I tried, I was told I could enter, but from here I would not be able to return from it. So, I never tried it again. It's not my time yet, to know.

At the top of that tunnel and past the faces, you will run into one to three full figure souls. They extend their arms out to you to welcome your journey into it, except for one, who is holding a rock tablet. It appears to be so heavy, and yet, he is holding it with such ease. This soul was the one, each time, who told me I was not allowed to enter, and the last time, he told me that if I do enter it now, I could not return from it, back to my present body. He does not judge you. He only allows you access, if you're ready. I have never tried since, even though I have seen the of tunnel open up, afterwards for others. as they pass on. I just cruise by it and smile. Each and every time I see the tunnel, it has always appeared to look the same, in almost every detail to my experiences of it.

Never worry about passing-on. There is a huge and beautiful world beyond the simple phase of physical life and you will always be helped by others, if you want to be helped. Your family will come to acceptance of your passing and life will still go on in the physical. If you are worried about seeing the moments of your family in their future, you are always connected to them through that vibrational link that I keep talking about it. You can see and even experience emotion with them in their future opportunities if you chose to watch over them.

Religion/Money/Tithing

Let's take a small break, and talk about religion again, as we know it. As I have mentioned, religion was formed to help our brothers and sisters try to unfold the knowledge and wisdom we already have but we were subsequently separated from the knowledge because of our emersion into the physical world. Our constant desire to feel and be one with the physical, has caused us to temporarily forget our true nature of, literally being, co-creators with God. Yes, we are co-creators, and can do anything, as our father, or God, can. This physical body of ours is simply a transport vehicle like a car. Once it is broken, then we can get another vehicle, if we choose.

Later on in our history, mostly of late, organized religion was created and was well-intentioned in the beginning, except they censored a lot of things in the Bible. The ancient religions didn't censor, and a lot of good information I am telling you now exists, and it will be found in time. It will be a real shock to organized religions around the world when they are revealed to all if organized religion still exists at that point. In relation to when, or how long that may take, when they will be discovered, I have a good idea, but not for me to say and may be in pieces here and there type of thing, at first.

I'm going to talk about the religions that most people know by their common name – Christianity, Catholics, Mormons, and Jews, Muslims and Jehovah's witnesses and many many others. Religion was never intended to be organized. However, now as it's evolved it has taken a lot away from its roots or the essence of religion.

Religion started out as individual with each individual helping others progress. Then, since organized religion has taken off, the Bible has been censored many times over (which saddens me). But the censorship started way before the Bible. So many sects and isms, of such, have expanded and continued to multiply. It's almost ridiculous now. Yes, individuals will always have different viewpoints, but that is not what religion is about. It's not to take an off branch and create another ism because they're viewpoints differ. Religion is supposed to be individual development. This is why there are so many sects and isms now.

One religion can be successful with one ideal that encompasses all viewpoints in relation to that one ideal. Most religions already have a few very basic ideas that they all agree on. The rest is just viewpoints. It's absurd to think how one religion is better than another. Is that not straight up public judgement or what? It's baffling. The very thing you teach and yet you so proudly use it to judge others with. It's just as bad as saying in the name of God we can kill, maime and rape you. Seriously, what the hell is that all about. How do you get others to believe that? Hint: We are all saved from our birth and on. No need to hurt somebody else in the name of God to be saved. You are already saved. Don't be brainwashed by somebody else! Think for yourself! No one is greater or better than another!

This is why religion must, and I stress again must, and needs to be individual, like it was supposed to be in the beginning. You can, and are, more than welcome, to have neutral houses of worship. No names given, sects or isms. Just neutrality of religion, so we can study our roots, back to the one and only God and we as co-creators with and part of Him.

I don't mean to offend anyone in religion at all, but I'm just simply observing what I see, and feel, around the world. Yes, which can be considered a judgment of, but it is of a neutral base. Your choices are your choices. I am in no position to tell you otherwise, for I am the same as you. It is difficult to describe what I see and understand and try to help others understand what I see without my own points of view and be considered neutral. To stay neutral it would be much harder to get others to change for the betterment of all and just start helping others, instead of themselves.

The only other way is to outright show so called "miracles" to others, which is only natural law, but even that, lots of people will skeptic the hell out of it to try to convince everybody it's fake or a trick. So that won't work anymore. I have always done them anonymously or tried, even though a few times it has been public, but luckily was probably shot down by critics. But, one shouldn't have the need to show these abilities to be considered seriously. This abilities are a natural extension of what we all can do.

The information I am giving to you is the information that the Bible and many other ancient text's was based on with all of the stories and parables of a brief history, of such, thrown into the Bible. You see, back then, just like today, what you don't understand, you change to fit the supposedly meaning or betterment of all. If it is not understood, or you don't like it, then you just omit it, for the supposedly betterment of all or do I dare say build a larger congregation.

My book was edited by others who also didn't understand the meaning of how I was using certain words and then omitted them and/or changed the meaning of the words to fit what they thought I was trying to say. So I had to go through and reverse what they had changed to the correct meanings.

What I see, especially in the Western world, but also in the Eastern world are religions that have the biggest congregations, with the most amounts of money collected, and creating the biggest places of worship that their money will allow. It's their show of strength and power hence their religion must be the correct religion to follow. It's becoming every bit as hypocritical as politics. Many sects that I can see and feel say; if you don't believe this way or that way, then you're going to hell – you need to believe what we believe, or you will be condemned to ever – lasting hell or have virgins at your passing.

I feel so much for those individuals. These religions have set individuals up to judge others, and use religion, in the name of God, to judge. It drives me crazy when I see this. Remember I can see into anyone's head, if I choose. Also when being around crowds it can be difficult, because of all of the judgmental thoughts people are thinking about each other. It horrifies me that many religions have turned this judgment into reality for its members, and the members don't even realize that they are judging, in the name of God, and it is okay to judge others, because it is, in God's name.

Especially, when members of organized religions, find out that you are not affiliated with a religion. The judgments fly then in their heads. Like, oh, my gosh, it's a sinner and they are going to go to hell if I don't try to help them. I've seen many remarks like this. I have even sat back and watched two different affiliated religions come across each another and they judge each other in their heads basically saying our religion is the correct one over the others. It's crazy.

I would like to see what many Western and certain European religions are going to say, when several scrolls and stones are found showing evidence of re-incarnation, no heaven or hell, as they teach it, karma based theories, and how judgment of others really backfires. I'll be watching, witnessing. This is what religions are based on, and those items are their scapegoats of why they want you to believe that what they are saying is true. But it's not, it's a fabrication, generated from fear and they call you a sinner.

The money thing with churches has always irritated me, as well. I understand enough to pay for your staff, helpers, and a place of modest prayer. But, remember religions are forgetting, that all is taken care of and will be provided for if you are genuine. It's a basic law that works continually without fail for everybody, business and countries. I have seen and felt religions using their money, investing in other things that they condemn, to make more money for their religions, and calling it good and necessary. Any divine religion will have no need to require their sustenance of money to survive. They will be provided for – have Faith!

People will give out of gratitude, and there will always be a way given to survive. All will be given unto them. Money has been used to simply be an excuse of many religions and teachings to survive and live in luxury, as in the ten percent of your earnings. To me that is stealing and disrespectful. Basically you are a thief! I, as well as many others, already know and have experienced, if your intentions are true, you will always be taken care of.

They bring up that saying in the Bible to give to others and turned it into helping them or you will be a sinner and will go to hell.

In this day of age, especially with what the IRS and other countries give religions huge amounts of leeway as far as tax free and tax deductible. If you are truly legit - why would you have to buy a plane, car or even a house? Do you not think members or even rich members could provide this for the benefit of the write off to help you? Yes, it might not be a top end jet, maybe just a regular plane that would work, or be just a basic or even nice car you can drive yourself around in instead of a limo to drive around in or even a big house or mansion. Isn't that what you're teaching? Or is the excuses is because you are so busy you don't have time to drive yourself and need to fly as fast as you can to meet others throughout the states and world to help them? What is the hurry? To help others with limited time or keep chasing the more money? I'm just curious? You don't need this extra money for yourself. You could put it out to help even more people, instead of yourself? Am I right or wrong? If you want nice things for yourself then why are you using the name of religion to do so? Be a salesman somewhere else please.

I realize most of the world and religions will fight this and say our world in the present can't run that way. It can and will with true faith. Believe in the physical and yes, it won't work. The physical lacks faith. It's easier in the present day times to pull off than in the times of Jesus, and He even said the same thing back then. Like FEAR, any reason of why not, is just another excuse of your own fears!

You might not live in a big mansion, and have acres of religious buildings to show off your religion or seat more members; But, that's all against the origins of religion, anyway. I used to read the Bible when I was younger, but there aren't even enough true sayings, word for word, from Jesus himself or others, that equals more than ten percent of the Bible. It's all censored by the various religions of its original conception to work for the benefit of organized religions. Yes, I dare say this, because this is the truth.

You see, the information I get is received in as clear and concise language and wording, that the authors of the Bible tried to imitate. I can easily read through the Bible, and tell you exactly what is given from Him and what has been filled in, and/or misinterpreted by others. It's the same source so it's easy to recognize. It is such a shame that censorship and misunderstanding has caused so much misguided philanthropy, in the name, of that good book and may other books of various religions. The ideals of the book, are excellent and good natured to all though. It has also helped millions of people towards believing in the one God or source and this is good too.

Remember, this one thought. Would your money given to your Church be better spent on the Church or to a homeless individual who needs food and/

or shelter in their present moment? Or a single mother or father just trying to survive and provide a life for their child. What you give to your Church could help another out for an entire day or a week or more. Which one would be more beneficial? Your money and help can be given to anyone to help them. They don't have to be homeless. They could be somebody who has lost their job with a family and is struggling to pay their bills or put food on the table. There are multi-millions of families throughout the world in need. Just reach out and offer your assistance without wanting repayment. This money tithing is just like the creation of the Devil and hell to scare you into repentance which requires money. It's all about getting that money to survive. Guess what, you won't have that guilty feeling of not giving to the Church hanging on you either.

One Religion

There are good religions out there, and there are a lot of sects and isms, who are trying to genuinely help others, and do the best that they can, for others. They get it. I'm simply trying to wake up the majority of organized religions of the world. I will give you a great challenge to all major organized religions, sect, and isms of the world. This challenge I'm going to present they must accept, or most religions will fall out of being. It's already happening worldwide. So, if your religion is so important to you, this is what you must do, and must do soon, because karmic ties have been set, and are starting to take their hold on organized religion. So do or become history, it's up to you. The world will be watching.

I've heard what I am about to tell you, is of the anti-Christ saying. I'm telling you now that the anti-Christ saying is simply a defense mechanism, to preserve what they have – their scapegoat – which they won't have soon. And I have one question of you to the various religions out there. How would you know if it was the anti-Christ or not? Really do they have a sign saying, "Hello I'm the anti-Christ?" The much more important question I have for you is, WOULD YOU KNOW IF JESUS WAS BEFORE YOU, RIGHT IN FRONT OF YOU?"

Do you think Jesus would say, Hello, I am Jesus, Son of God and the world would just believe Him? The world would look at Him as being just another delusional person, unless He decided to show off some of His abilities. Even, then there would still be skeptics from all over the world trying their best to disprove it. So why would He pronounce it to the world or would he just be and let others decide for themselves? Realize, as Jesus has said, I am the Son of God - we are all the same. We are Sons and Daughters of God. There isn't one specific person who is from God!

My ultimate challenge to all religions of the world, "IS JOIN AS ONE. " Forget the names you go by and the books you use, and just join as one religion, in neutrality with the only goal being towards helping anybody in their advancement of awakening, back to their origins of the one God and us as co-creators of that one God. If you want to be graced by karma, and truly help others, this is what you must do, or fade away. It's your choice! This applies to all religions presently and in the future to be.

If this is to be, remember this: Keep one set of ideals that everybody can agree upon. Like God is the only God or source of all. Then treat others as you would like to be treated and do not judge others or become judged yourself. This will work, if egos and judgments are laid aside for the common good, which is possible and don't try to over organize it. Keep the organization of such, as limited, as possible. I didn't say this would be easy! This will be nearly almost impossible in its current state, but it is still possible.

Now, if we took only the major religions of the world, and not counting all of the sects and isms, which actually comprise a big part of religion too, imagine the power that it would have. It would be bigger than any governmental entity in the world, and possibly even greater than all governments combined.

If religions joined together, they could wipe out almost every major problem we have in the world. They could even "strong arm" politics, in a peaceful manner, one through democratic vote's, to make real changes in the world. No other entity in the world can do this. This is why I hope to see these mentioned changes occur, sooner or later, and unite. So much wasted money and energy in having different perspectives and fighting each other.

What could religions do if they became one? Religions could wipe-out hunger throughout the world, so no soul would experience starvation ever again. One religion could wipe-out worldwide homelessness, and create millions of jobs. They might even be able to stop wars and have free quality healthcare world wide?

Remember, help others to receive what they feel, they must receive, and through understanding, they will come to understand themselves and will help others too. Keep that from them, and it will only prolong the experience required, and drag-out karma. So love your enemies as you love your family. It's a must if you want to achieve and know what true forgiveness is! An eye for an eye will only consume itself. The pattern has to stop eventually.

One religion could help fund, and bypass the big private companies that lobby, and help bring alternative energy sources to the forefront in all categories. Many, if not, hundreds exist, but money has been used to bury, and push away most of these alternatives, until they benefit them, and it will take a lot of money and power to get around these private industries.

Trust me, the time has come for karma, and its effects have started to hinder these profiteers and lobbyists, considerably. This is the perfect time in our history where all things should start to culminate toward positive change. In fact, universal change for the betterment of all souls. I emphasize again, THIS IS THE TIME for change just as it was two thousand years ago. If we don't, then we will flounder on, as usual, and go further into our karmic debts, as a society. We have some very big natural phenomena coming our way that we have created with ourselves with our greed's of the world. We must get a long for once and deal with what's ahead of us. If we work together the next century possibly two will be a lot easier for society to tackle.

If we stay scattered and separate, the next two to three centuries are really going to be harsh to deal with.

So I am saying again, "We all need to get along." Quit judging each other! Treat others as you would like to be treated. Helping others is absolutely crucial! I can't stress this enough! All violence of every kind was created by us through us from lacking to help and treat others the same. If we treated everybody the same, as brothers and sisters, crime of every kind would be non-existent. It's favoring another or taking advantage of another that has created all of this. This trend must start to reverse or a leveling will be at hand. So I ask of everybody to help reverse this trend, even if others have done wrong to you. We need to forgive everybody. Then a greater challenge can be taken. Help those that have done you wrong! This is the test of true forgiveness. Not just say you forgive them, but then help them if they need it. They are doing wrong because they probably have been wronged against themselves and trying to exact revenge or act out because of it. Remember this statement to yourself: "Father forgive them for they don't know what they have done." Everybody is at a different stage in their spiritual awakening. But, all need to be forgiven in the same manner.

The "Way" the "Pattern" the "Example" was given, but the understandings, of such, was not fully understood. This time it is for the kindness, compassion, understanding and forgiveness for EACH OTHER.

Aspects of Karma

Let's continue on with our discussion of karma and encompass a wider range of its infinite aspects. I will discuss the various subjects of: General karma, reversal of karma through grace, seclusion, abortion, politics, suicide, genders, vanity and wars.

First, let's say you are a racist. Racism is a very good and an obvious example. Say, you don't like people who have a different skin color than yours. You avoid them. You try to stay away from them, and make fun of them, by calling them names or worse. By not treating others as you would like to be treated, and judging them through their skin color. Why in the world do we care what color somebody is? Are they less educated or perhaps even more educated? What is the fear of this in this day of age? If people of color had the power in the past, then it would be the color of white which would be racist against. It was simply a power thing back in the past. We need to see past this point. What happens if you ever see an alien? I don't think they are going to be looking very white? Are we going to be racist against them? Just because they are different?

For starters, just thinking these thoughts alone, you have created a judgment to come your way. So, people will think the same of you. Second, if you act these thoughts out, the same will probably be brought back unto you. Maybe not in this lifetime, but in the next, you will come back as what you have judged and face the same thing. Be a racist and you will come back as what you have judged!

Women! Just like racism why does this still even exist? How is a women less than a man? The only thing a man has over a woman is physical strength. What good is that used for? I think of everything we have today of convenience, luxury and technological advancement in every way has been created by intelligence and not strength. O, but we do have sports that we can beat each other up with or out do the others in performance. Yes, they can be emotional, but that's all it is. Emotional! That must be why men are better than women. They can beat each other up better than a woman can? We are stronger than they are? The control thing. In the past needed for protection, like an animal, now not, so much.

It amazes me sometimes our logic and we call ourselves advanced. With technology, technically women don't even need men anymore and they could live on and help the species survive. Can a man say that? Perhaps, we have this backwards. Man always chases and needs woman. Why? As a guy I know why. We are driven just like an animal by it. We need it and want it, but we can't have it without them. We need them which scares us. So since we are stronger then we should control them simply over this one thing. Yes, that makes a lot of sense. So if it is so desired to have a woman, even in Muslim countries then why are we condemning them for it? FEAR!!! Fear of perhaps, they are better than we are overall? Just a thought. If I have this correct, yes man can control a woman physically, but does that honestly make you more superior to them? If it does, then basically we are a lot like the animal kingdom. We don't think we just react, fight and control. Where is that going to lead us?

Lie and cheat to others, for whatever reason, and be ready to expect the same thing, in return. You lie and cheat over your own FEARS! Cheat on your spouse, and be ready to be "cheated upon". Put a gender down, and you will experience the same in return. Beat others and you will be beaten. You've heard the saying, live by the sword, and die by the sword? This endless cycle can come to a halt and reverse through kindness and understanding – which leads to grace and forgiveness. We must end this repeating cycle.

We all know the consequences of smoking, taking drugs (even prescription), alcohol, food, gambling, sex, vanity and etc. They create habitual and/or mechanical overindulgences of the physical desires. Karma involving indulgences causes fast ill-effects of the physical body. Generally, within the same life time. The reason is because your actions or over indulgences bring on direct karma unto yourself versus to others. I'm not saying enjoyment of such is bad, we are here to experience and enjoy. It's the over indulgences that will bring consequences.

You see, karma begins with your thoughts. If you have harmful, judgmental or any negative thoughts towards another, you will receive those same types of thoughts from others. To eliminate this, this mentally, is the hardest too eliminate, because people are used to having privacy with their thoughts. You can think it, but not speak it. Hmmm

You must start to catch these thoughts, from the start. When you feel racist towards somebody, catch yourself, in your thoughts from putting them down, or judging them on their style of clothing, tattoos, hair styles, body piercings or whatever. When you catch that thought, ask yourself, why am I thinking this way towards this person? I don't even know them. They have their own circumstances that they are dealing with. Then stop your thought, this is the first step in stopping and reversing the process. The second step is to understand, why you are having these thoughts. Most likely, they are first based upon how you were raised, and then of your environmental factors and/or your urgings may have been drawn from your previous lives. Were you brought up this way to judge others? Was it correct? Did you grow up in a neighborhood that made you judge others? Was this correct? Maybe this is a great test given to yourself?

Through oneness, you can discover your past lives, and see why you are judgmental, and have certain fears and aversions to certain things and situations. Another hint of previous lives is seeing what you're urgings, or desires, are drawn to? Do you like oriental items, Egyptian items, civil war items, renaissance era, medieval things, horses, clothing fads, colors you like, likes and dislikes, subjects you learn very easily in school, arts you're attracted to, etc. These things and a lot more are all hints of what and where you have lived before in previous lives. You can have anywhere from a few to lots of urgings and/or gifts– such as perhaps being a genius, in certain areas. All of your abilities – whether progressive or hindrance of, follow you, until you release yourself from all attachments. To me a born genius is a pretty obvious explanation of it. If you keep doing the same thing over and over and over repeatedly, you naturally become extremely good at what it is. Your memories and experiences follow you. You can bury them or like most young kids they don't know how to bury them so they show what they can do.

You can also use this method to compare to your relationship with another. Do you like the same things and/or the same areas of interest? If they are the same, you and your other probably at least knew each other from before in the same era or location and may have been married before.

Another of one's own past lives is, if you have a common face or you hear a lot, "You look familiar," as people call it; it's not because of your physical make-up. It's your soul recognizing another soul from a past life. So when people make comments to you like, "You look familiar," and you know that you haven't seen them before, it's because your soul has recognized their soul. I get this all of the time wherever I go.

I give a challenge out to those individuals who have chosen to live in seclusion of the world – monks, etc. I understand coming to know thyself, and some try to stay away from life, to avoid its supposed temptations. As, I mentioned earlier, if you don't put your understanding into use, as in sharing with others outside your family and friends, you will lose remembrance of your knowledge, and location which through karma has been happening to those in intentional seclusion. In some of my previous lives, I have been many types of religious figures. So I understand seclusion, in trying to know thyself to know God. My challenge to you is simply to go out into the world and share your knowledge and wisdom with others, outside of your seclusion. Help others learn about themselves. Remember, know thyself is only one aspect. Helping others is another one – a very important one. Through helping others you can challenge yourself to a much greater degree, and increase your spiritual awakening and opportunities for increased awakening. Not to mention the world is a great place to test your attachments to various emotions, desires (ego), and materialism. You can like and enjoy this attachments in moderation and yet maintain an un-attachment to all of them. It's a great test to test yourself.

Karma is starting to force you outside yourself. Go out into the world and share your knowledge and your heritage will survive. Don't, and eventually, you'll be forced out, and you will then be forced into a new location in an opportunity given to learn from and not repeat. This pattern has come up before may times in the past, but it won't stop until you interact with the public and help others with your understandings.

Okay, understandings once you figure out why you are judging within yourself, take a look at the person. Don't judge, but ask yourself, "Why are they this way or that way?" You might not know this right away or possibly ever. But, you are setting up in your thoughts to get rid of judgments and replacing them with understanding. With practice and patience, you can come to have your answers in regards to understanding. I will talk about this later on in the book.

If you're acting these judgments out, stop and look at yourself first, before you act out. Say unto yourself, am I better than they are? And I don't mean with your education, knowledge, money, physical given labels or in any other way, except that they are an individual soul, just the same as you are. They have their karmic ties that they need to release and gain understanding from, just as you do. They have their circumstances to deal with it just like you do. Once you come to understand this, judging others will start to fade away, and after awhile you will automatically stop being judgmental to others, and come to understand their circumstances that they live, or have lived.

When understanding is reached over and over again, the grace of karma is given, and the cycle of "an eye for an eye" type of karma, goes away. You see, grace is the only law through which karma can be released without having to go through another experience of the vicious cycle of judging, whereby that particular karma can be ended, and the true understanding of awakening, can be achieved. Say you take another's life; you could end-up repeating the experience of your life being taken, until you come into the correct understanding of why it is wrong to take another's life.

This next area of karma that I am going to talk about can be extremely hard for most people to understand. But, if you see what I see this is how it truly works. I can see it and feel it going on everywhere I go. This is where it's important to remember, love your enemies and forgiveness will be given.

Again, let's study racism for a moment. Whatever they do to another, they will come back as the same as they have judged, and be judged in the same manner that they judged the other, to help them come to understanding. The one giving the judgment back to the other may be a soul brought back to help the other soul experience and understand from it. Remember, these bodies of ours should be viewed as vehicles. They have a purpose and can be discarded and brought back again through a different vehicle. This applies to murder, rape, kidnapping, theft, pedophile crimes, etc.

You see, since all energy and God is of neutral progressive energy there is no such thing as good and bad, only awakening or becoming more emerged, in the physical senses. Which do you want to do? I realize this is very difficult to understand with genocide, wars, rape and child crimes. Once you truly come to understand that our bodies really mean nothing to our beings, and then you will actually come to understand the beauty of our physical bodies, and everything physical. As mentioned above with genocide and/or child crimes i.e. – victims and victimizers – it takes two to create these scenarios. It takes two to tango.

I realize, in the physical this is truly hard to understand. If I see somebody being injured I will step in to stop it. If I see another shooting others I will step in to stop it whether I am armed or not. There is instant karma that can be played out in these scenario's too. So you don't have to be just a witness to it - you can act against it! I, personally am not going to stand around and watch another person get inured in some way. That is not who I am. So you have to be realistic and have common sense with this stuff in the physical, as well. Perhaps, one was killed because it was their time because of the arrangement they had made previously so they can move on to their next experiences.

Understand, before we are born into another physical body, like the beginnings of our dreams, we analyze our previous lives, reactions to situations we dealt with, towards the awakening of our soul. Once we have reviewed this information we think about it, and try to come up with our understanding of it. We have other souls help us to review our life, to help us understand. At this point, you try to understand the why's of our decisions. Once you feel that you are ready to redo these situations, and take on more growth opportunities for your awakening, you will be ready to go.

Then you will start to look around at appropriate surroundings and you're soon to be parents. With karmic ties, generally, the same family members will hang around each other until their karmic ties are forgiven, or worked out. Roles can reverse, such as the father can become the son, or the daughter becomes the mother. The possibilities are endless. Some souls are looking for surroundings to experience or work out, so their parents are of little concern to them. So as, soon as they are allowed to leave their parents control, they are off to experience what they have set out originally to accomplish. You look for parents that would best suit you, genetically, to accomplish what you need and the surroundings that they are around. You see, our physical bodies are simply bodies to experiment with, and unfold with – to our advancement or further emersion into the physical. It's as if you are looking to buy a new car with all the different options and customization to choose from that will better serve you.

Some more advanced souls or old souls, let's call them, can come back to help parents experience loss and such things. When souls return in a handicapped form, it is, generally to see what and how their parents are going to deal with and experience their child's handicaps. It is difficult for souls to awaken and experience when a body is mentally over-incapacitated, but the soul knows, and the subconscious remembers. So in a situation like this, the older soul is simply helping the other soul (s) for their experience of it. There really isn't much of a gain for the older soul.

I'm sure you have heard of people calling other people an old soul, or a young soul. I personally see it when I look into somebody's eyes. All it is is really how awakened one is spiritually. Generally speaking it does follow how many times you have been reincarnated, but doesn't have to. Just in the general natural flow of it the more times you have been re-incarnated the smarter with common sense and calm you are. You've been there and done that and did this and that and learned that was not good or was turned out good. Or I'm sure you have seen kids and young adults who are well beyond there years in their demeanor, experience, knowledge and the way they act and react to situations. Far ahead or very mature for their age.

Younger souls tend to get into a lot of trouble because everything is new and they don't have a lot of consequences hit them back yet like a child. Middle aged souls tend to be very curious. Therapists, psychologists, priest/ pastor and politicians are good examples of this - teenagers. Trying to figure out things and how we work. Middle to older tend to be more enforcement type, protect others, help others, doctors and willing to die for others - parents. The older one's are more like grandparents. A teacher, social worker, nurses, doctors is a good example of them. They will help you in any way they can. They have the experience, the money and knowledge. Then you have the ones who are much rarer to come across. They are the some of the oldest., perhaps the most stubborn or gluten for punishment? They are all about helping others, sacrifice themselves if needed for the benefit of another, spiritual awakening and etc. They can be anything, but usually very modest in what they do as a living. Live simple lives without drama. Always calm no matter what it is. If you look into their eyes you can just see and feel the oldness, wisdom, experience, lack of fear, and probably piercing eyes looking thru you.

Some karmic conditions maybe that you might have injured others in a certain way in the past; therefore, you will come back experiencing what you had injured, or done, to others.

I, personally, was one of those that had my own plans, but I tried to do my best with parents. I respected and listened to them, and they have been great parents. Through oneness, which my parents don't realize either, is that I was able to recall the first time that protection of myself also included protecting my mother went into effect. My mom was six or seven months pregnant with me, when my mother and I were almost killed in a car accident with a huge dump truck in Naples, Italy. I can remember a big loud crash, and crunching and although my mother did not scream, but cringed throughout her body in fear. I then felt a big push come out from us towards the noise, and then the noise stopped. We were almost crushed by a huge dump truck. Now I understand it was energy pushing outward. One of those Angels I have talked about.

My wife always wanted a daughter first. So my oldest daughter arrived first as a talented writer and reader. With our second child we waited nearly four years, before he was ready to return. One night I told my wife, you are now pregnant and he is going to be a boy. Nine months later he was born. I had talked to my son in the fourth dimension five times before he was ready to be born again. I was expecting him to be ready to be born in 1998, but he said, he still had some things that he wanted to work on first before his return in two thousand. Our third child, our daughter, was a gift to both of us, and she has her own plans of what she wants to do.

I cannot mention babies and pregnancies, without, bringing up the hot topic of abortion. Again, another subject I'm amazed in this day of age we still can't agree on or figure out! Souls can take possession of a fetus from anywhere from the time of conception, up to one month after a baby is born. If a soul sees that a body is going to be discarded, or be incapacitated without a purpose, it will not take the body, unless it's an advanced soul who has chosen this body to help others around them to help them deal with understanding, of patience and forgiveness. A physical body cannot live past one month old, without a soul taking possession of it. Remember, our bodies are rechargeable batteries. A new body can only sustain itself on nutrition and fluids for a month before the conscious will no longer function. Medical science can keep a body going for years, but the soul still has to be there for any spark to happen. So a soul is still there even in coma. Years don't matter to a soul. Now is the soul occupying the body 24/7. Definitely not. It might come back here and there for a few minutes and that's it if your in a coma state. No reason, to hang out there or need to energize the body much.

So I ask of you, how is abortion wrong? What are you disposing of? Physical flesh like organs we eat, blood transfusions, fish, meat on animals and chickens eggs? Just like a genetically –cloned body will not survive, if a soul refuses to accept it. Or is it over because religion has told you it is wrong? It's not in the Bible, so what religion told you so? Abortion, obviously existed back then too. Or is it back to since a man doesn't have the final say in whether to keep it or not because it's not in the man? It's purely up to the woman and the man can't handle that?

If you want to make a real difference with abortion, this is what you must do. The most important thing in this abortion debate is judgment. Ask yourself, who are you to judge another soul who is the same as yourself? Again, sounds a lot like the male over women control issue and religion telling you its bad again. Gender is of no concern on this subject. If you would like to win this debate then don't judge another. If you judge them you will be judged in the same fashion by them. It's a vicious cycle you just keep continuing on with judgment of each other over this debate, and it won't go away until you stop judging each other over it. I see it all the time with people over various heated subjects throughout the world, just watching the energy build and swirl around their thoughts, and just building the karma thereof. Do not judge! Let it go, through understanding and forgiveness. The best thing you can do is to help them. Provide safe care, medical attention if needed and help with it. As you would want for yourself.

Let this be a warning to you: Judge somebody on abortion and there is an excellent chance you will come back and be in the same circumstances as what you have judged! Yes, we can switch genders no problem. Sometimes, it takes a couple to a few lifetimes to get used to being the other gender. This is where gay and transgender categories come in.

Let's talk about another heated subject. I'll even give you the solution to this one. With this one, keep in mind that this one solution could solve a lot of problems within the world on other subjects if handled in the same manner. I rarely, give direct answers to influence future changes needed. Generally, it's up to society as a whole to decide, but here we go.

Immigration! We have had problems with immigration for thousands of years throughout the world. Why? It is simply over greed, selfishness and fear over survival. It has nothing to do with helping your brother and sister souls, our own brethren. Absolutely, nothing. It's a big shame just like starvation, homelessness and medical care. Neither needs to be felt by any soul. Borders are just like racism, except the immigrates, we say, take the jobs and create crime and etc. At least, that is what we are saying about it and yes it's true to a small degree – our scapegoat and they might be, but we have created those circumstances for them. They want to survive and provide for their families, as anyone does. Put yourself in their shoes or circumstances. What would you do for yourself and your family? They are looked down upon by others and then shuffled and kicked out as in an exclusive club. If doesn't benefit them, then leave them type of attitude. Since they are not welcomed by others, they react to our reactions, thus our current problems.

We have created this upon ourselves, just like gangs, organized crime and terrorism. We all created this through our selfishness, greed and not helping our fellow souls. Remember, kindness and forgiveness crushes hindrance. Now we must suffer a little to restore balance again. A leveling must take place! If we can't do this ourselves, karma will eventually handle it for us. We have had four previous re-starts as I will call them. Which karma has been warning us on and not too far off, will make it a five.

The solution, remove all borders throughout the world. Why is one country better than another, if that other country could help other countries citizens out? Why not? In time, this action would balance or level out equivalence to all and bring equal opportunities to all and actually help each country financially. It's always over land, money and resources that each has more over another, in some cases a legacy that lost land and is trying to regain its prominence again. Look at oil. How many wars have we had over oil? If we continue to keep borders throughout the world and keep others out, we will continue to have problems with immigration and it will never be solved in any other manner. Remember, karma? Look at what we could do with that money, time and resources spent in trying to stop it and put it towards helping others. If we had all had one religion to follow, then religious issues between other countries wouldn't exist either. Ego's.

Immigrants must also be willing to conform to whatever country they are moving too, also. Be respectful of those countries customs and language. Try to live in the way that they live. Don't try to force your beliefs or language on another country. It goes two ways to be successful. Be thankful for the future opportunity. If you don't like then you can always go back to the country you came from? I think you will realize it's better not too, so you get frustrated at where you come from and take it out on the country that is actually making it better for you overall.

Remember the golden rules: Treat others as you would like to be treated, judge and be judged and through helping others you will come to know God and yourself. These laws must be followed and can apply to any century of our existence. They apply forever and can be lived out forever. Any excuses, otherwise is due to fear and not following the words given unto everybody.

Each significant meeting with another, who you have a significant connection with, or you are, or were, have even possibly fallen in love with, is filled with karmic cohesion. These relationships are very important connections. You could have been married before, had a quick affair, boyfriend/girlfriend, etc. Unless all karmic problems have been resolved, these connections are repeated opportunities for the both of you to resolve your differences. If you have had a really bad relationship with say, an ex-wife or ex-husband, you might as well plan on meeting again to reconcile your differences. Remember, you must learn to get along and not judge each other. Remember, patience and understanding takes time to truly come to forgiveness. You cannot run away from your fears or issues.

Jobs, everybody has their own job or lack of job. Everybody is individual trying to make their way. Do not judge another on the job they have. Do not look down on them. If you do and it's a pretty consistent attitude you have. Guess what? You will come back just as how you have judged so you can understand what it feels like.

Now let's move on to politics with karma. Politics is actually going down a very leery path right now and has been for a while. Taxes are increasing for people, and spending is so far out of hand by most governments! They're only saving grace anymore is to tax more on everything, and create more laws to do so and restrict freedoms. They are desperate right now. The governments of the world need to downsize their control over their countries.

People don't want, nor do they like, big governments. Big governments are a serious drain on their citizens, and eventually, it leads to a Communist and/or a Socialist type of control to survive. Keep this in mind to all governments. Your citizens are paying for your government and positions. Not because they choose to, because by laws they are forced into. That is already a bad scenario. Forcing others to pay for your benefit. We are not here to be taxed. We are here to awaken ourselves through our freedoms and experiences – not to be limited by others over materialism and power. Taxation on purchases is a much better and equivalent method for fairness to all.

The way politics and governments have grown in all aspects everywhere, karma is now coming back to those built up systems, and is starting to break these systems down due their greed and power, just like organized religion. No one political organization or country, has ever survived because of this. But, right now we are peaking in an extraordinary way with this greed, lying and power. Changes must be made soon, or it will get worse because the survival mode will kick in with politics for their greed and power. Anything they can do to maintain their positions and power.

Campaigns are a perfect example of judging each other. Each different party and candidate finds everything they can bad and use it publically to hurt the other party or candidate. Most people are sick of this. It is so distasteful and it reflects our own political systems in place. Then we vote on these individuals berating each other. Isn't that ridiculous? Be respectful to each other and don't try to outdo the other. Just a radical idea here, but what if each candidate tried to show the best of all of their competitors qualifications and then let the people decide? It would require and use a lot less money to campaign, as well.

Politics should be for the people, not the money. The people shouldn't have to run through years of hoops to get some agenda approved for the betterment of the people. Hint: For our politicians be very careful of how far you take taxes. Keep in mind; remember a few hundred years ago. When governments drained their people with taxes and increased laws to hamper their freedoms. The citizens began to move away.

Keep the people strong, and the country will remain strong. Abuse the people, and eventually, you will falter. I like the tiny cities and countries that have no or very little taxation and laws. They breed success. People are not here to be taxed, and kept down through financial hardships. Estate taxes are also ridiculous! Help spur the economy by ridding yourselves of estate taxes. Estate tax shows disrespect to your citizens. Estate taxes have no value to its citizens, only to the governments and states. It is only brought on to help governmental bodies, only. It is selfish and greedy.

One other question for politics since it is driven for the people. People are always frustrated, because they know their taxes are going to pay for the less privileged or lazy to work as some call them, which we have created. Did you know your taxes pay for all of the politics going on, including the entitlement of Congress and other groups of entitlement? We are all paying for Congress and other entitlement positions for their entire life. Not until they get a new job or position, but for their life. That same amount of money could pay for hundreds of families within a single year for every year. Have we the people voted to pay them their entitlements for life with our tax money? Just like a regime. Let's re-examine all monies paid to politics and then vote on what is appropriate and what is excessive. Just an idea? Maybe reset the way we conduct politics. Maybe one government name versus republican and democratic to oppose each other, which creates judgment of each other, instead of working together for a common goal. Just like religion, it sets each other up to judge each other from the beginning instead of working together. Why can't one body have differing opinions and come to a conclusion, instead of two doing the same thing and just fighting each other over everything.

Once again, just imagine how much money and resources would be saved in combining political parties, instead of fighting each other? Less positions needed, less paperwork (more trees saved), saved time and increased efficiency. Not to mention all of that money saved. That money alone could probably wipeout unemployment or homelessness, eliminate starvation in the United States, improve our education system, pay teachers more money, maybe pay our deficit off, free health care and etc. It could be equivalent of what it costs to support a war? Wouldn't this be better for all versus the few? If politics don't take action on this and other various spending, entitlement and use of your own for their few, karma will level or eliminate it in time. Karma has already started to kick in on politics, just like we have been warned with Louisiana, shifting poles, bigger floods and more fires. There is always a pattern in nature. There are always warnings before it really gets ugly. Wouldn't it be nice if we fixed the problem first, before karma has to fix it for us?

Enough of politics, let's talk about karma with suicide. Suicide is not a solution. Just because you have the free will to end your physical body before its time is up, doesn't mean that all of your problems will go away. Remember, there is nothing on this earth, or any other dimension that one is given, that one cannot deal with. Think about it this way. You end your life now; later your same circumstances will come back to you again in almost the same type of situation and circumstances. Suicide practically mimics itself again and again, down to the details, so you will have to confront and deal with your situation sometime. So just deal with what is given onto you in the now, so you can move on with your spiritual awakening. Remember, maybe you have created these same circumstances onto someone else and you are simply paying for the karmic debt to them? So understand, its' subtle temptation to end problems, only to repeat them over and over, until you confront it and conquer it.

Gender. Most souls tend to keep in the original gender, throughout most of their reincarnations. The male is active and women are passive energy wise. Each soul decides which gender will benefit them more in their spiritual awakening. The gender can be switched if the soul believes it will be more beneficial to them, or have to play out a karmic debt against the other gender, which most of have done.

Now with attraction; active and passive energy or forces are attracted to each other, as in male and female. Just like you have your mommy's little boys, and daddy's little girls; it's all in the energy. This energy helps to comfort one through helping each other complete itself as a circle, until one becomes their own circle. It even applies to those who like the same sex. There is still one active energy and one passive energy. It can also be said, that the human body whether male or female is beautiful in of itself.

Those souls that are attracted to the same sex are generally from younger souls. They are still trying to decide which gender will be more beneficial for them. Judge and be judged. But, the law of energy attraction still applies. One is active, while the other is more passive. Sometimes one has switched genders is because they have judged the other gender before and are simply experiencing what they have judged before. Just like abortion, you judge it to the extreme, and you will become what you have judged before. Your choice. Or you can simply understand it now, and let those individuals live their life as any other soul would without interference and/or judgment. Both genders have their positives. Which one you prefer is more of a matter of what you are trying to achieve with their awakening. Do Not Judge over this! It's a basic experience I can almost guarantee we have all experienced in being both sex's. Which sex you prefer or both is simply an expression of or experience for one's self.

Vanity. Vanity can be good as in regards to hygiene. If you have taken good care of your body and appearance in your previous lives, then you have a good chance of being attractive and in good health in your future incarnations. Unless, you judge others as comparing them to yourself or somebody else and looking down or acting upon them. If you have and still do this, you have opened the door to your experiencing the same in return. If put down others down for being overweight or having certain physical disabilities. Once again, you have opened the door to your experiencing the same in return. Everybody is good as they are! No need to change anything. Just be the unique you are as everybody is.

It amazes me how society picks out really good looking people then tries to change themselves to look like them? Why? In the near future it is going to be a lot easier to do this, but why? Then it would be like seeing the same people over and over all of the world. Then everybody would be tired of looking at it. Do you not want to be unique or just the same as somebody else? To me love is in uniqueness of another.

Don't worry about aging. Aging is natural. If you want to keep more of your youthfulness then know thyself, help others, don't worry about anything, and let your spiritual forces unfold. It's not an instant answer, but by far a much better option. Yes, science will figure this out with immortality, but it still won't stop others from passing on in unlimited ways of passing on. Nature will always keep science guessing and advancing further. Hint: A natural law of all physical life - is that all life will recycle! It's a guarantee. From black holes to nature itself. Every little bug and animal has its purpose for recycling. Even if you imprinted our minds onto a computer eventually it will become corrupt and break down. Recycling is inevitable.

Big business has the same type of karma. If a business is started and kept in line with its highest motives and ideals for helping others, then it will succeed. If the motives falter, due to greed and power, the business will fail.

Currently, it has become quite obvious, in witnessing what big businesses have done, and have become, through having too much greed. The only way to overcome this is to go back to your motives, get ready for the hits which you must take to make amends, and start again with what you have left. Repeat this greed again, and more than likely, the business will not be able to survive. If you have a big business, then scale down your investors a little and do more good with less quantity, i.e. "less is more." You are being given the opportunity to help others. The more responsibility you have been given the more opportunities you will have to help others. Abuse this and you will become abused yourself.

Business also has a 2 way street with karma. It's just not about the business, but the people. When you work for a company try your best. Don't use the companies rules or policies to your benefit. They are there to help you when you need it. Meaning don't be lazy and work slower to get paid more, or use unemployment for other reasons, help each other, try to help the business perform better - they did give you a job right? So don't try to use that against them and hurt the business. This also creates karma which will come back to you. If you're lazy and drag things out for your own benefit everybody sees it. So nobody likes you unless they are the same way. So now you feel as if nobody likes you. You have created this! Cheat the company and the company knows this and they can't wait to let you go. Then you will blame them for letting you go.

Karma also applies to wars. If countries fight and have wars, hopefully, while believing they all have good intentions, for their people, and they aren't fighting over power, resources and greed. The war will end swiftly with minimal casualties. If it's over failed perceptions of one or both, lies, land, hint legacy and resources then it's going to be bloody and long. It's rarer to see wars over legacy, but as history has shown us many times over - this generally leads to even more reduced legacy of land, huge casualties over ego and resources over time. Every country who has tried to take over other countries eventually ends up with even less than they had before.

There are so many aspects and pieces of karma to take into consideration. I have only highlighted the general overall categories in my book for you to get the idea about karma. One could write an entire book on karma alone. Hopefully, with the explanation's I have given to you with karma, you will now understand karma and how it affects every aspect of your life, your significant other's life, your neighbor, employer, state, country and the entire world as one society.

So start with your thoughts. From your thoughts just be kind and helpful to anyone you come across that needs a little help. This starts to create an awesome cycle of goodness.

Oneness and Intuition

As I have mentioned, oneness is the key to most of my abilities and oneness enhances every ability I have. Remember everything I can do, you can do and more. This isn't some saying. That is reality. So let's start talking about the abilities that we all do have. Remember this: Psychic abilities are a natural progression of one's soul development and awakenings. The more awaken you are to everything around you, the greater and more psychic abilities and all other abilities you will have. Everybody is born with them awaiting to unlock them. Just like our memories of everything is there even down to the cells, but locked away until you decide to awake them. Some genius's have unlocked them at birth in certain areas as an example or can be unlocked later on in life.

Intuition is the most reliable, most natural gift we have – it works whether we want it to or not, and it is very efficient and will never steer us, in the wrong direction.

Intuition comes directly from within you, from your soul. It comes in many forms. Most of these forms you should recognize. Gut feelings, something that doesn't feel good or look right, hairs stick up on your skin, suspicions, and hunches are all examples. Your own intuition starts from when you awake from your dreams in the morning, until you go to bed at night. It never stops working for your benefit and growth. It is you. A sixth sense, so to speak, that you need to recognize and utilize more for yourself, as well as for others, in all walks of life.

You see, your soul has to experience the physical third dimension within a body, because your own soul is, and operates at much higher vibrations, than that of the physical. However, it has chosen to experience the physical. This is achieved through the soul first having a "middle man," more commonly referred to as, the subconscious. Our subconscious is our recorder and translator. The next is our conscious mind, which houses all of our senses and is the physical mind of the body. The subconscious remembers everything between the conscious mind and the soul, and then interprets information between the two, because the vibrations between the conscious mind and our soul can't feel or understand what each other are actually experiencing.

Every single thought whether acted on, or not, is recorded in the subconscious mind, including the soul's impressions to be sent to the conscious mind. Your conscious or physical mind can easily miss details, while your subconscious records every sense you experience plus records every detail that your physical eyes can see. Every detail is too much for the conscious to take in and process with a focus. Every minute detail down to every blade of grass on a lawn, for example. Understand the subconscious mind is neutral and very powerful, and this is why hypnosis works so well. It's the same concept that I use consciously, when I talk or send messages to others. I bypass their conscious mind, and send messages to their subconscious mind, to get to their soul. It can be difficult for the conscious mind to interpret messages from the soul although it does but not through physical words, unless you become advanced and/or sensitive enough. You can set aside the conscious mind, as I can and anyone can, but at first, you must recognize when it is giving you hints and warnings. This is what I want you to develop first and foremost, then advance, if you so choose. Listen and/or feel those hunches you get and it can be over anything just not bad stuff. It is working 24/7 for you. You just have to get sensitive to it and then with more and more practice with it, it can and will become second nature to you. You will start using without even realizing you are using it anymore.

Hypnosis/Conscious Mind

Let's interject hypnosis first. Hypnosis works because our conscious mind only interprets senses and images. Our actual thoughts all thoughts are housed and recorded in our subconscious. Granted the conscious mind retains memories, but can lose their memories with physical degeneration. So hypnosis moves past the conscious mind to talk directly to the subconscious mind. Imagery, emotions, and all senses felt by the conscious mind are played out in the subconscious mind. All of our thoughts are from the subconscious mind, except our reactionary memories of the physical. Then the conscious mind simply acts it out in the physical body. This is why you can play back situations and/or memories from hypnosis.

I, myself, send or talk to others directly through their conscious mind to their subconscious mind. I learned early on that having a normal conversation with somebody consciously, they just do nothing and they generally don't truly grab what I am talking to them about spiritual conversations, but by directing my language past their conscious mind, their subconscious mind picks it up directly, gets the message, and passes it on to the soul. Remember, I can see other's thoughts move around. I can see if this process has worked or not, and that's how I figured it out, by seeing what worked and didn't work.

I personally have never tried hypnosis, but perhaps someday I will try self-hypnosis to see if I can gain more complete details about the workings of everything. Maybe, someday. The reason I don't is because at this time in this life of mine, I prefer to have full control through my consciousness.

Now I can receive any and most information from vibrations around us while being fully conscious. This is what psychics tend to do. They are sensitive to the vibrations around them and around others. Anybody who wants to learn about hypnosis or self-hypnosis, which I prefer for others, you should study the books of Edgar Cayce. In my opinion, he was a master at self-hypnosis. Remember, when I said, that I quit reading books on all of the subjects of the spiritual and paranormal, because they were all outdated for me, except books on Edgar Cayce. The first book I read from Edgar Cayce, it blew me away. My information mirrored his information in text, ideals to a degree and sometimes in language or grammar. I was fascinated by that. So I started to ask questions about Cayce. I remembered that Cayce and I have had many good conversations together in the fourth dimension over spirituality. I hold high regards to Cayce and as a friend. His ideals are of the highest.

Tuning Intuition/Telepathic Communication/ Intuition

Now, back to intuition. When you're in a difficult situation, feel the emotion, or gut feeling you were feeling first, before you even have another thought about it. If you feel that something isn't going right, or isn't going to go right, that's your intuition, or soul trying to communicate with you giving you hints of how you should react to whatever the situation. But, keep in mind this thought is before your conscious thought. Your conscious mind uses logic and organization. Your soul can't talk directly to your conscious mind with its vibrations, so it sends images and/or feelings into your subconscious mind. Then your subconscious mind tries to bypass your conscious mind with hunches and feelings. So if it feels wrong, it probably is. If it feels immoral and/or wrong to do something to another, then don't do it. If it feels right, then by all means, go for it. Or conscious minds are built for the physical world. It's not built to handle vibrations from the soul.

The more you use your intuition, the better and easier it will become to use and understand your correct feelings from intuition. You see, it might take you awhile to get used to your feelings in regards to what feels right and feels wrong. Initially, your conscious mind tries to interpret the language from the subconscious interpretations from the soul and can blur the correct message. In time, you will learn your own way of bypassing your conscious mind and the first initial thought or feeling will be correct. Not the questioning of it that the conscious mind will naturally do. My second guesses are usually wrong thus my conscious mind has convinced me other wise to chose the second. So as soon as I figure what the conscious mind picks I then remember what was the first choice that came up for me. That is what I will choose.

You could try your intuition on cards for practice. Just lay a card face down and guess its color, first. When you can do this repeatedly, say seven to eight times out of ten, you will be getting your intuition down. Then try the suits of the cards, and then the numbers. Or drive your car into an area that you don't know. Drive and make turns down streets, letting your intuition help guide you to find your way out, but you have to say to yourself your looking for the exit. Let your intuition say make a right or left or drive straight. Or try the popular corn field mazes. Do not look at the map given – just rush in, and let your intuition guide you without giving your conscious mind the time to react and think about which way to turn. This is one way I trained my children when we do them to help develop their intuition. My oldest picked this up very quickly with intuition. In a grocery store, think of an item you want, and let your intuition guide you to it. Just keep imaging the item in your mind and tell yourself, lead me to it. Or have a friend hide an item in the house, and let your intuition guide you to the item.

Then you can start to use your intuition, to start to figure out what people are going to do, and are thinking. First try to feel what they are feeling about you and others around you. This is easier to learn before you try to read their thoughts. Emotion is a easier gateway to read others thoughts. Eventually with practice with feelings you will gradually start to pick up on people's thoughts naturally. Just like older married couples can just know what the other is thinking. Overtime they have learned their partner's vibrational link of thinking and the obvious of knowing each other's patterns.

With others thoughts, images, pictures and sometimes a word or two will just, "pop" into your head. You'll get to know, if you don't know already the difference between your thoughts and thoughts that have just, "popped" in. Now reading of one's thoughts is simply becoming one with the person. This is why feeling their emotions first, is easier to get before their thoughts. But, when you connect emotionally to an individual then their thoughts will then start to transfer over to you.

The other way is more intentional mind reading. This is what I do when I want to dig into one's thoughts to get to their soul. I look directly into their eyes. Almost as if you are pushing thru and past their eyes. From here, I will see thoughts and I can continue to go past until I see blank openness. Then I have connected to your soul directly. From here, I am automatically tied to your soul. I feel, not see your soul's thoughts, feelings and original ideals for this current life. I feel how you have reacted to situations in the past and present. This is how I get to know your soul. If you don't reach the soul part you can still pick up on images, symbols and glimpses of information. You see people think with images and pictures, not words.

Through oneness, all you have to do is glance into another's eyes to get the same results. You can also heal others with a glance into their eyes, as well in oneness. Just remember, mind reading is all about being in tune with another. That is all that is needed. Oneness, of course, makes this connection very easy. You can practice with a friend and family too. But, beware if it does work, you could pick up on thoughts or images that you would prefer not to see. This is why I don't really use it with my family and friends.

Have a friend read a book or think about an object or concept. Then the other will try to feel or tap into that person while the other is having these thoughts. Distance doesn't matter. They can be right in front of you to countries apart from you. Remember, that vibrational link? If you don't pick up on the idea right away that your friend or family has, then have the friend or family member give you a small hint or hints until you can pick up on it. These will probably be a must to get these down if you have never attempted mind reading before. But, that is perfectly okay. Just like using your intuition to guess cards. Little by little you will improve with less and less hints, until no hints are given. Then you've got it and it will only improve with time.

Things to remember with mind reading. For one you rarely get full complete sentences or even words from people. People don't think in full sentences when they are talking. In our minds is an image and our conscious mind turns that image into words for us. So you would only pick up on bits of words but mostly images of what they are thinking about. Our minds don't like language. Our minds like pictures and images and this is what you will see most of the time and their concepts of their ideas. Now when they stop to think about something or an idea during a conversation, then you can pick up on those thoughts. This is also a good time to send messages into their subconscious because their conscious mind is side tracked with trying to recall.

It has always fascinated me that we have all of these different spoken languages and when you tap into somebody's thoughts you don't even see the language only the pictures and images in their head. When somebody talks somehow the conscious mind takes that image, scenario or picture and turns it into verbal language within a fraction of second. It is just so incredibly fast and second nature to it. It's quite amazing. So fast that it is rare you actually pick up on a word or sentence from somebody unless they are seeing the word of sentence as an image. Then you will see it. Even if it is judging another you still see more the picture than the words, but it is easier to see words when people are talking to themselves inside their heads in being quiet. Its as if the language is being spelled out in the brain like an image, so it's easier to see words then.

If I have a very easy connection with somebody, I can ask them a question or about an event or a book. I then look into their eyes and extract the ideas of the question, event or what a book was on. This method is very fast. I can extract this information within seconds, instead of having a dialogue about the question, event or book that can last for several minutes. I used to do this with my oldest daughter, but definitely with strangers too.

Once you start to pick the thoughts up of others. You will only get or see images at first. Glimpses of thoughts, pictures and rarely actual words or language, this is where you begin to read the thoughts of others. From here, it will become easier and easier to get more complete thoughts and images. At this point, you will also start to begin to get thoughts hidden from their childhood to present. This is where anything can of their thoughts pop into your head, so to speak. This is why, I always ask somebody before I go this far into their mind, because I never know what information will come to me. It can be embarrassing to discover intimate thoughts, desires, and what they like and what they wore including their underwear from the day or week before. Nothing is hidden from you. This is where your intentions must be of the highest. You just never know what image, situation or desire they will bring up to their conscious mind. Our minds are truly astonishing in how incredibly fast it is with a multitude of things at once.

The more you practice these methods, the more using your intuition will become second-nature to you. Then others feelings and thoughts will become second-nature to you, as well as their body and facial expressions. I use my intuition everywhere, and in almost, any situation I run into. You see, your intuition has access to all and any information all of the time even into your on going future, and now you are simply learning to hear, see and feel this information, through your conscious mind. I stress again, that this is the best and purest information you can get, because it's you from your soul.

The calmer you are overall, the better and more efficient your intuition can come through you. If you are a person of lots of drama and or keep yourself very busy in life, you are almost intentionally ignoring all intuition and basing everything off emotion and experiences. So in life don't worry about situations. There is always an answer. Just remember, if you need hints to calm yourself, and sense more of what "oneness" feels like-look to nature. This is what attracted us to it in the first place, to emerge into it. Nature is pure neutral energy, in motion. It just flows, living and progressing forward, throughout all of its trials, tribulations, and distresses, and it just keeps moving forward in perfect harmony. Our souls see this in motion in nature and thus, this is why we are so attracted to it. We can learn from nature.

The movie "Phenomenon" with John Travolta, was a good example of this. The movie when it came out struck a big chord with me. At this time in my life, this is what I was experiencing with all of the continuous information I was receiving, and coming to understand. Then I too turned to nature like he did in the movie and then saw the pattern of life just gently flowing along completely calm no matter what it went through. That's when I truly came to understand calmness. I learned it before I saw the movie, so it kinda of hit me, I wonder who or how they figured this out because it is so true.

There are other sources for receiving information. If your intentions are for the good and pure, you will not have problems. If your intentions are self-involved and/or self-driven, you can have problems. For example, the Ouija board, automatic writing, tarot, etc. These methods do work, but are driven by neutral energy. So there are souls in the fourth dimension that are still trying to remember things about their spiritual awakening. Just as most in the third dimension, they will throw out answers and try to trick you just for fun. Your intentions have attracted them, so they decide to go with it and play back.

Telepathy. Telepathy is simply the connecting of one wave length or vibration between two people or more, and knowing each other's thoughts, on that particular wave length. There are several ways to communicate between each other. The simple basic communication is for you and a friend to set a time and day, for thirty days in a row, to connect to each other's wave length. Each of you clear your thoughts, and one of you thinks of one object, for a few minutes, particularly if they have a picture or are drawing a picture of some sort. Then their mind is more concentrated on the picture, instead of wandering around with other thoughts at the same time. During those few minutes using imagery, (which I personally prefer for me), think of that one object being directed, or transported to your friends head. Your friend will imagine that he/she is transporting themselves into the others head, trying to see what the object is. Then you and your friend both write down, or draw the object. Do this and you will come to know, basic telepathy.

Telepathy simply works by tuning into certain vibrations. Once you tune into that vibration, you can get almost any information you want. You can tune into anything, anybody, living or not. Everything has a vibration(wave length)

One way to tune into certain vibration's, is to imagine the person, plant, tree, rock, or country as a whole, and simply concentrate over and over on it, until you start to feel what's going on with them or it. Once you can feel them or it, then the rest will follow.

When I use this method I only need two things. A picture of the individual or thing, if one is available, or to see the individual's eyes, in person or through a picture. In person, I need them to ask me only one question from them to be guided into their thoughts for a particular answer, although those thoughts can come running forward from them before I can ask the question. The question can be anything, the question simply directs their thoughts towards me so I can grab that vibrational link.

Or usually, I just look at a picture, and can tell you all about them. Through consciousness it is harder to get exact dates and numbers, but everything else is fairly easy. The reason exact dates and numbers are hard to pinpoint exactly – is because the translation between the conscious mind and subconscious mind gets jumbled, with numbers and dates with frames of time. Your conscious mind is driven by senses and images. Senses and images aren't stamped with dates, per sa, unless you have memorized the date with the image, then you can get the exact date, because you have memorized the date like an image. Now if your' under hypnosis or self-hypnosis induced your dates and numbers can be exact, because the conscious mind is bypassed. That's one of the flaws of using conscious control.

Others can do the same thing through smell and touch. Those that prefer to touch are simply tuning into the vibrations of an individual or an individual's items. This is the same method I use, but through pictures. The effects are the same. Once you tune in, it is up to you how far you want to connect with that energy, or vibration with them. For example, say the person is currently in a state-of-depression. You can connect emotionally with that individual, in any state of mind that they are in, and feel what they feel, as if it were happening to you. I generally keep myself separate from this part, unless, I need to break into an individual to help them. Psychics do the same thing, but they are tuning into you, the individual, and connecting to your vibration of you or the memory of somebody in question. This is possible because everybody is connected and can connect to the vibrational link that I have talked about.

I'll give another effect of telepathy and oneness. Eventually, when you get good at this, which anybody can (it's in our nature). You will be able to pick-up on all kinds of thoughts going-on in another's head, and they may not always be nice thoughts. You will see so much of that, that this can become, overwhelming and disappointing to you in how others judge each other. A lot of times, if they can see you, they will also have judgments towards you. This is why, judgment of others, is so big for me to highlight for others, and hopefully, break down as much and often as I can. Big crowds will become a nuisance to you. Trust me, once you get to this point you will truly look at us as humans in a different light. There is a huge amount of negativity, shame, jealousy, hatred, lack of self confidence and etc going on in people's heads. It's actually more of a surprise to see a person who is having positive and happy thoughts.

There are many ways this information will come to you; by images, words, sentences, and feelings from others. When I am in a crowd, I get bombarded, with all of these thoughts pouring into my head, from every direction. At first, it is cool, and then it becomes very tiring, after a while, unless you tune it down and focus more on the physical experience as everybody else is doing.

Negative thoughts take more energy to create than positive thoughts. Negative thoughts tend to drain others around them to maintain the thoughts. The positive thoughts tend to give energy out to others around them and you gain energy back to yourself. That's why nobody likes being around a negative person and generally everybody likes being around a happy person. It just feels better and more uplifting than being pulled down by the negative person.

To block images, when I am in a crowd, or don't want any information from individual's, or my family, I intentionally think of another subject, at the same time that I am talking to them, and I avoid direct eye contact. That way if I look away or not directly into their eyes, then I don't tap-into them accidently. Now with my family members it has become second nature to me to just block them. When I look into my wife's eyes I see the physical eye and the beauty in here versus going past the eye. So just viewing the eye as a normal physical eye turns that tapping off for me.

Tapping into individuals has become so second-nature to me, that I have to intentionally block myself from peeking into other people's minds. When you tune into others, either intentionally, or by accident, it can become so natural for you, you not only tap into their present thoughts, but a lot more of their hidden thoughts come out. You see, when you first tap into somebody, you will see images, pictures and scenario's of what is currently in their thoughts. You will gain all of this information with a single glimpse. Then that glimpse passes, and you start to pick-up, a lot of off-the-wall, information. Their information can be picked-up instantly from their childhood, any experiences where they've had trauma, you will see images of the things they like, including their desires, wants and needs, including and not limited to sexual desires, and past experiences with other lives. Nothing is kept secret from you, within a simple glimpse, once you have tapped-in.

In the past, when individual's have asked me to see what they are thinking about, I have come to learn to ask; are you sure you really want me to tap into your thoughts, because I won't just pick-up on your current thought, but any thought you have in there. It's difficult for others to hold onto just one thought at a time. Yes, you can do it for a few seconds, but then your mind goes onto to other things. The conscious mind is very busy at picking up all kinds of signals from its senses then add memory and reactions to that.

The more secret an image is, the more they bring it up in their mind to try to hide. It is kind of ironic. Think about what you don't want me to know about. To prove this to others, I have given them their current thought, plus I start to add some embarrassing intimate details to show them, they can be an open book to me. It is very difficult for me to lie to others. So if I'm not being bold and straight up, as I usually do. I try to be nice and dance around the answer to comfort them, instead of telling them the answer straight up. I've tried to lie to others before, as we all have, and I'm really bad at it. Every time I have tried, I can just look into the other's eyes and see that their soul knows otherwise. Consciously, the individual might not pick up on it, but their soul and everybody's soul knows when one is lying or being truthful. It's in our nature just like intuition.

I've had individuals pick their favorite number or a particular number, or image they like. The problem with this is that number and image can change within that moment. You say, pick a number, and only think of that number up to one hundred. Instantly their thoughts scan several numbers, until they pick the number they like. If they hold that image in their head, the number is easy. But, most of the time they don't. Usually, they will think of another number, or two, that they seem to like also, and then, you have their thoughts come in as well. They generally think, how can he see my number, and what else can he see besides that number. As soon as that later thought comes in, a flood of quick embarrassing images pours in, and then back to the number they were supposed to be thinking about.

Science is correct with body language and facial expressions. With seeing images and thoughts from others and comparing them too obvious body and facial language, as science describes is true. Body language and facial expressions coincide very well. Usually body language happens before the thought is present. Body language is so second nature to us in speed the same as us talking with language. It's just so incredibly a fraction of a second.

Another method of telepathy is tuning into the subconscious vibration of every soul, who is present, in the third and fourth dimension. Tuning-in to that one wave length or vibration that connects to everybody's subconscious thoughts and memories. This is the method that Edgar Cayce generally used, when he conducted his readings. He would hit this vibration, and "zoom," he went off to locating or finding where the individual was at the present time who had asked for the reading. Edgar Cayce gave readings for most people when they were in other states or countries. Generally never present in front of Edgar. This method is harder to conduct when you're still in the conscious state. Unconsciously, this method is ideal. Only need a little guidance to find who you are trying to locate or information you are trying to discover.

I prefer my conscious state, so when I hit this vibration, I only pick-up images, feelings, and thoughts of the individual. Consciously, I cannot give word for word verbatim, because my conscious mind is still intact and trying to organize the information to make more sense for itself. I generally use this method for more of an overall view, on current, past, or future things to come. Such as, I can feel what governments are doing overall, or how countries are doing – financially, morally, or how they're people feel about their country overall. I also use this method to tap into how the Earth is doing in its patterns of evolution. I will tell you now, that we are not hurting the Earth. The Earth has plenty of time to fix whatever we are doing to it. We as a global society are only hurting ourselves, with the changes that we continue to do to the Earth. I can also feel and see upcoming weather and Earth changes. Anybody can see and feel what I can see and feel.

I'll give you some prophecies at the end of this book. Everybody seems to always be drawn to wanting to know the future. One only has to release their doubts and fears, and they're longings for these things, will end. You'll just enjoy life, the way it is supposed to be, moment by moment. You see, wanting to know the future, comes from lack of self-confidence in yourself and greed to make more money or insecurity of your life. So just release you're worries and enjoy life and whatever opportunities it brings. Every day you are given opportunities, and take those opportunities, as positive steps to your awakening.

Telepathy can also be used to locate anything. For example, my dad enjoys going hunting. He will open up a map for me, and tell me what he is hunting. I'll look at the map, and I can tell him, when, where, how many, how big and small, and what time frames, that, for instance elk or deer, will be cruising by or the paths they will be taking, in certain areas all within seconds. The same thing with fishing, except he will, only give me the name of the lake or reservoir. From that, I can tell him where the best fishing spots will be or whether it is going to be a bad day for fishing. Just for fun, I can tell you where any oil reserves, fresh water reserves, gold, silver, natural gas, bodies or anything; you are looking for, simply by looking at a map. This method of telepathy is a lot like remote viewing, which I will talk about in my next chapter.

Continued and advancing use of telepathy will eventually lead you to touching on oneness. You will be able to achieve oneness, and be able to tune into everything around you, including inanimate objects that are available for you to tune into. All energy patterns of everything you can see, hear, smell and feel, mix together, just as a dog's nose creates images in their head without even seeing the person or object. Then you will come to know the truth about physicality. It is only one-big giant illusion of happenings, and supposed experiences, that are perceived to be real.

Remote Viewing/Astral Travel

This takes me to my next area of remote viewing and astral traveling. There really is no difference between remote viewing and astral travel, except remote viewing is more sensing a place or person's particular vibration, while astral traveling is actually the movement of your soul exiting your body and traveling to the place or person. Remote viewing is what governments used to employ to attempt to spy on each other and gain access to un-accessible areas with various governments. Astral traveling is freer traveling without intentions of where to travel to.

Remote viewing is achieved through meditation and using your conscious mind with imagery. Remote viewing is the ability to get information about an unseen person, place or object through your senses or imagery. Remote viewing is what I do with maps and pictures of individuals. It's all about hitting that vibrational link.

The basics of it: You mediate as usual. Get yourself calm and using imagery, you pick a place or person of interest to you. For example, I would pick a place like another room in your house or where your office is that you work. While meditating think of the place you're planning on visiting. Keep imagining that place or person. Then boom you automatically connect to the vibrational link and now you can describe what you are seeing and feeling. This is remote viewing. With remote viewing the information can come to you through thoughts, images and senses of what you're looking at, whether it is emotions of the person or place to facts and desires. I say looking at, but it's more of sensing it that translates to images in your mind. In remote viewing you are not traveling there, but hitting the vibrational link. To travel there would be astral traveling. Then you can actually see images firsthand.

The other option to remote viewing is astral travel. Astral travel is basically the same thing as remote viewing, except you imagine your soul or soul body rising out of your body. With astral travel you only need a general area you would like to travel to. With astral travel you can see your surroundings as you travel to anywhere on the Earth and beyond. Remote viewing you only sense a specific place of interest and its surroundings only. Remote viewing you can see a diagram of a building or map and ride the vibrational link to it and describe it. Astral travel you are literally traveling.

To achieve astral traveling try it with meditation. Once you are calm and relaxed, through conscious imagery, you imagine yourself lifting from your body. The lifting can be from anywhere, your head, back, front, or wherever. Keep imagining this thought, and then when you feel you are ready, open your eyes. If achieved, your physical eyes won't open, but your eyes of your soul will. If achieved, you can be floating above your body, or be completely somewhere else, where you can't see your physical body. This takes some practice to achieve consciously.

Every time, you go to sleep, your soul automatically lifts from your physical body and cruises around, mostly in the fourth dimension or spirit world which is simply the space between it all (dark energy). The first time you achieve astral traveling while remaining conscious, you will probably freak out, and then all of a sudden, be looking back through your own physical eyes. You see, when you and/or your soul, leaves your physical body, your conscious mind is still in control of your physical body, and your conscious mind is always prone to lean on its survival mode, of the physical body through its senses. So when you achieve astral travel, perhaps you do freak out, these thoughts are coming from your subconscious mind, which then triggers your conscious mind into its survival mode, and boom, you are back into your body in your protection mode.

When you're astral traveling, and your physical body becomes disturbed – through sound or touch, your body will go into survival mode, to protect itself and, boom, you will be brought back, in a fraction of a second, to your body. In astral travel your soul is doing the moving and your subconscious becomes your thoughts. Remember that black energy (I talked about) that interconnects everything in the third and fourth dimension. This is where your soul travels, and is found in the black energy. You can cruise around the world, and see whatever you want to see, and faster than superman, if you want to.

With astral travel you can travel anywhere within the third and/or fourth dimensions. So during your astral traveling, your subconscious remembers all of the information that you were seeing while traveling. Your imagination is your only limit to your travels. We all do this in an unconscious way, every night when we go to sleep. Our soul leaves and goes cruising around, but most of us don't remember, its journeys. You can ask yourself before you fall asleep to to remember those memories of where your soul goes for you. It might just work for you.

It's a lot of information for the conscious mind to deal with and accept. The conscious mind can seem to feel inferior and locked up, so the subconscious mind blocks those very experiences from the conscious mind (ego), unless you have learned to calm your conscious mind. When your conscious mind is calmed you can remember anything and everything within your conscious thoughts. The thoughts won't be memorized only come in from the subconscious so it doesn't effect the conscious mind. Your ego becomes aware of its place and purpose.

Your soul leaves your body many many times throughout your day, without your being consciously aware of it. If you are doing a lot of repetitious chores or work, daydreaming our soul will tend to leave your body more than if you are constantly throwing different opportunities at it for spiritual growth and awakening.

One really big hint that I have learned through astral travel and being consciously aware of my soul is that when I astral travel, all colors and images around me, are much more vivid and sharp just like my dreams are. So consciously, I see my alarm clock or any image that has bright colors especially electronic items or even nature and because my soul is more attracted to those vibrations of electricity, the colors will stand out more vividly and brighter, and are in much sharper focus. This is how I can tell throughout the day when my soul is back in my body. When I look around at nature or electronic items, and they appear much brighter and sharper than normal, I know my soul has returned from its traveling. That is when I know, at that exact moment that my soul is looking through, my physical eyes. Usually when I am helping somebody with their spiritual growth my soul is generally around when I am talking to them. Another way I always know is by my energy levels in my body. They will be much stronger and much more sensitive to everything around me.

Your soul can hang around from most of the day to only a few hours of a day. I've tested this with watching objects. As soon as my soul is back, all objects have a greater color and detail to them. Then I can be looking at the same object, and it will become dull again, when my soul leaves. This is simply a curiosity or effect that I have figured out over the years. Your soul looking through your eyes is a very subtle change, but if you are aware you can come to notice the same thing. I've also noticed that when I talk to others about growing spiritually my eye color tends to turn from a very dark blue to a piercing steel grey color. This is what others have told me. After seeing this, I can see why others have told me over and over that when they look at my eyes that it looks like I am looking right through them.

I'm sure you have heard of medical patients, who were being operated on, and consciously they were sedated, and yet during the operation, they watched their doctors perform their entire surgery. On being revived physically, they were able to give in detail what their doctors did to them and maybe even what they talked about. They were in astral travel mode, and generally before these patients went under, they had a deep desire and/or concern to keep an eye on their doctors, during their operation. So their subconscious mind relayed the message to their soul, hence, they observed their desired effect of.

Anybody can do this consciously. We do this every time we go to sleep unconsciously. A fine and small line between the two. It's simply a matter of being open to it and taking action towards it. Try it, you might like it.

Energy/Auras

Auras and energy. Aura is the energy field that every soul gives off, as spent energy. Think of it as a fire in a fireplace. The wood would be the soul and the physical body would be the fire. Science can easily detect the heat given off, but not the vibrational energy given off as flames. Kirean photographs can take images of these energies or flames of, if you are curious. Everything radiates spent and used energy into another form of energy. Energy can never be destroyed only transform. It's mind blowing when you really think about it. Energy is forever like us.

There are many different colors in the flame depending upon what material the wood is burning. This is the same with the various colors that we give off with our physical body and soul every moment we have a physical body that a soul is occupying. The greater your spiritual awakening or wood, as in the example, the brighter, more light, and more energy you will give off. Some people can physically see, these colors emitted from others. These energy colors emitted are originated from light within ourselves.

I, myself, can only see these aura colors, when I change my vibrations. I don't see them every day, - all day - , as some people can. But I do know that an indication of what people wear, is an indication of the colors that their soul emanates. Any color blue is always good, especially dark blue (the darker the blue, the more balanced overall you are, and the closer you are to spiritual enlightenment). People who wear dark blues are generally very relaxed and calm about themselves and their surroundings.

Green is an interesting color. It's not an overall color as in blue or other colors. It's generally mixed into their main color. The more green you have in your aura at times the more natural ability you have in healing others. But green as with the myriad of any of the other colors, can change within your aura. Green like the red color can be sporadic, in your aura. For example, when I consciously decide to heal somebody, in any aspect, the green in my aura jumps significantly in my aura colors, except when I decide to instantly heal then it's more white overall.

Red (which is only mixed in with other colors as highlights) always indicates anger. These people generally are always, angry at life.

Yellow indicates youngness and immaturity – younger souls.

Browns are more in the yellow category, except that they appear to enjoy life, and make fun of life, as in comedy. Browns are mixed with yellows. A neat color in my opinion. Laughter is always good for you.

Oranges indicates vibrancy and enjoyment of life.

Purples indicate they have the ideal of spiritual awakening, but are still young in their development of it.

The color black is harder to see, because it is mixed in, with other colors. It is usually mixed in with dark blue colors, and hard to see. One side effect of black is generally somebody is trying to hide something from others. So black, psychology wise, others feel more hidden, mysterious and the ego feels more empowered with the color of black. Black also indicates one who is spiritual in nature, but yet striving for the maturity of white.

Black and white is very neutral and can be hard to see colors, until they dominate your other colors. When you advance enough, dark blues become black and white mixed into the dark blue color.

The color white indicates maturity of spiritual awakening. One can go back and forth from dark blues, and whites. Sometimes, black can come into it. My aura colors change daily, as most others do, to a degree. It simply depends upon the task at hand that I choose to accept. If you look at my clothes in my closet, there is a very obvious theme. Dark blues and whites mostly, with other dark colors, such as black and such. I personally give off very deep blues, almost black with white flashes. More white is present depending upon the level of oneness I am in, at that particular time. The one exception is when I choose to instantly heal others. Most of my aura will emanate white, especially at my head and hands.

White, if present, tends to be more present in the head and hands of individuals, but generally, is in very small flashes. If you were in perfect spiritual awakening, you would be in complete oneness with everything around you, all of the time. You would emanate white from your head and hands, as your body would be more invisible or transparent white.

Grey colors indicate sickness, or internal illness usually within the physical body. It's a color I try to stay away from because I realize if I'm attracted to it or it looks good on me then I have got some internal issues going on that should probably be looked at.

No aura around somebody means their soul has exited from their body, and their body will soon pass-on. Some are very soon up to 3 days to pass-on the physical body.

Now anybody can wear clothing to duplicate their supposed colors, but your true color, is what you are attracted to, comfortable with personally. For example, when you see somebody in a certain color and that color just looks right, looks good on them. This is their true color. If the clothing color just doesn't look right on them then they are trying to change their aura color to something it is not. Like intuition, if you listen to it it's right. If you don't and your conscious mind makes the decision then it looks off, not right or fake even.

I'm sure there are a lot of other books on auras that you can read on this subject, for more details than I can give you. I only give you what I know and not from other books.

Energy/Pure Energy

Now on to the energy behind aura's, and all life. I could probably write an entire book on this subject alone, but I will just touch on the major highlights, at this time. Everything in every dimension or realm and every physicality is made of pure energy. Energy can never be destroyed, only change forms. Energy is the perfect example of your co-creation abilities, with God. If you can see energy patterns, you will come to see what I see. This energy isn't the aura energy I talked about previously. This is the wood that flames come from, so to speak.

When I heal, specifically, it is like the movie, "Matrix", again another movie that took me by surprise when I saw the ending with energy he was able to see. I was like where did they come up with this? Because that is very close to what I can see in people and everything. It's actually more of a continuous even flow, like that of water or the wind though, unless there is a break in the energy pattern. Then you can see energy bumping off an area like a broken bone. I actually see these energy patterns moving around inside people, within their bodies.

In oneness, you can see these same energy patterns in everything. How they flow in our bodies, and in animals, plants, trees, the air we breathe, and all inanimate objects. If you ever come to see this, then you will come to completely agree with me, that all of this is just an illusion or giant play for us, to experience, in understanding. Watching the movie "Matrix" was quite interesting for me. The closest version I have ever seen of what I see. Every step you take bends and blends into the energy below your foot. Your arms and body create swirl patterns while blending in slightly with the air around you.

In oneness, you blend in with this energy. Remember, your body is basically a rechargeable battery with its acids and bases. Your soul can draw on this, and any energy around it. In oneness, your energy is exchanged, to help whatever or whoever is around you, in need of energy. You will never run out of energy, and you can only absorb so much energy. If you absorb too much energy, you will give up your body and your body will simply disappear. This is why I am careful with my energy. I can push these levels, and I still have a lot to do before I check out.

This energy is the energy that connects all. It's the little black energy that is between everything. Atoms, particles, protons and neutrons that all spin around in it – within it. Here's a little secret. Everything acts and progresses in a circle or rotary pattern. Everything! This is a key for scientists. Change your focus from linear, and concentrate on circles. Circles are of the natural primitive laws, in motion. Just think of electricity and anything that creates electricity. Electricity is simply one of the byproducts of this energy (the black invisible energy). Imagine atomic energy simply comes from atoms and particles, which is still the byproduct, of the energy I am talking about. Even fusion which is greater than atomic energy, is still small in comparison to the black invisible energy that connects all. Fusion would be the equivalence of steam coming from hot water. Water would be the true source. Energy is completely neutral.

Thought and action are created through this energy. This same energy is what our souls are made of, and thus our creator. (Remember, as a battery your body reacts as a battery charger, as well. You can charge others up, including little tricks, like draining and recharging your electronic devices, watches and others around you. Do not try to intentionally drain others around you. You can, but you will drain more of their negative than positive energy).

Now how does this energy move around, and how do we absorb this energy, because this energy is what energizes our soul and physical body? This energy flows directly within our bodies, starting in our endocrine glands. I have read some books that talk about the seven chakras (basically, they are talking about your endocrine gland areas). Pretty good for back in the day, somebody must have been able to see energy patterns, as I can myself.

You see, your body brings energy in through these areas. From the glands, it goes out to our nerves within the body, and from there throughout our bloodstream, into everything else. These three areas: Endocrine glands, nerves, and blood, are the essentials of the body, while DNA is the creator of. Everything stems from these three areas. Study these areas, and you will discover most of your causes, including karmic ties (karmic conditions are brought on physically, within these three areas, as well). These areas are the creators and destroyers of everything within our body.

Organs are secondary, or more of an effect of these three areas. There is still a great deal to learn in these areas for science and medicine. Everybody absorbs this energy through their soul, even though most of us have no idea, that this is the case. You can absorb this energy consciously, if you choose, on top of unconsciously doing it on its own automatically. It does help the nourishment of your body and soul all at once. Your soul has a tendency to relax more, and not work as hard, so to speak, if you help it, and absorb some consciously. This is very refreshing to your body, and will help to re-balance your body, thus making you, more refreshed and allow you to enjoy life. You can absorb more energy by very simply meditating. This is why meditation is so comforting to you.

Most people have heard of the fountain of youth. This energy is, the fountain of youth, and can be used, as such, if your ideals are correct. Which if your ideals are correct, you will have no need for it. It will be automatic.

To absorb energy try to be in a mediative state first. Then open your hands and use trans-mediation to visual white energy or whatever color you want pouring into your hands like wind traveling into your hands. If it works you will feel your hands getting stronger, the muscles of your hands tensing up. Then you can tell and even feel that your hands are starting to become warmer and warmer and eventually hot. Sometimes, you can actually see a funnel of energy pouring into your hands. Your hands might actually move upwards feeling light in weight. It takes practice, but does work.

I, personally, just absorb this energy whenever I choose to consciously. Every time I heal, I absorb this energy automatically. As soon as I am ready to heal, this energy starts to automatically flow into my body through my hands.

Each endocrine gland has its importance and deals specifically with certain life awakenings that need to be mastered. I'm not going to tell you of each one's lessons. Find oneness, and you will find the answers to this. You see, if you concentrate on certain glands, over other glands, to help you learn those lessons over other lessons, (which you can do because of your free will), you will throw off the balance of your body and (you will experience ills from this). You do not want to create imbalances in your glands. They can mess a lot of things up in your physical body. Remember, patience conquers all. So if you choose to absorb energy, I want you to absorb and distribute energy, in balance. Oneness will distribute this energy correctly.

I will now tell you, how and where energy is absorbed, and where it flows. In oneness, energy can be absorbed into every pore and cell of your body, as it pours into you. This only happens when you are absorbing a lot of energy, at once. Normally, energy is brought in consciously through your hands and can circulate or exit from your feet. Your hands attract energy. Your hands will begin to heat up, and you can feel the energy out of nowhere pouring into your hands. From your hands the energy is directly reflected to your abdominal area.

Your abdominal area has the capacity to hold up to ninety percent of your energy, if it needs to. Your abdominal area is your distribution area. This is also where deep breath can be mixed with this energy i.e. meditation. From here you should let the energy flow where it is needed, which is where your abdominal area directs it to go. Everything has to flow through the abdominal area, and this is why the abdominal area is the distribution area.

Energy is distributed to the areas of the head – pineal, pituitary, hypothalamus. Throat – Thyroid and Parathyroid, chest – thymus, abdominal – adrenal and pancreas. Any disruptions or breaks I see, when I heal a persons' body, is what I am looking for to repair them. Due to this, I use my energy as a boost to help them absorb energy. This helps their bodies to heal, and get rid of and/or repair, if certain karmic conditions have been met.

With breaks in energy flows I have learned you can re-direct energy around them so the energy can still get through to heal. Breaks as I call them are more like a broken bone in imagery. The break is where the energy can't pass through or only some of it can jump over it while the rest gets kicked off to the side and dissipates. If you see this you can look for an alternative route as changing the route of the energy to the side and being able to cross over or around the break. This will allow for faster healing until the break is healed and the energy can smoothly go through it again.

Once our bodies have progressed or evolved enough to absorb energy more efficiently (which they will in the future). We will no longer have to depend upon food for the maintenance of our physical body. You can do this now in our current evolution, but until it evolves more in awakening and form, our physical bodies are still clumsy in absorbing and retaining energy efficiently. When this evolution comes, which it will, we will no longer need to sleep, or use physical language anymore either.

Energy/Psycho-Kinesis

Psycho-kinesis (in my opinion) is the ability to influence any energy form, to what you desire. In the mild manner of psycho-kinesis, you can influence, card games or dice games, these items of interest are very easy to influence. You see, everybody playing is already hoping to receive, draw, or roll certain numbers, or cards. The minute they hope, they flaw in their concept of life and energy. Hope, in and of itself, is fear and doubt. Though hoping to draw a certain card or number in dice, is the wrong way to go about it. By hoping, you will fail. not always, but the odds are against it. Hoping is very different than one having faith. Faith is having knowing behind it that it will work out. Hope is literally hoping that it will work out.

Now when I play cards or roll dice, in my mind, I already know, what the card or number is going to be. I don't do this all of the time, because I still like surprises. So when I can surprise myself, I do. Once again, I love imagery, so I automatically see the number or card in my head that I want, before I react. This may take a lot of practice, for some, while others will be able to pick it up almost naturally. Then you draw the card or roll the dice or whatever it is and it is expected to be what you have imagined it to be.

Confidence in yourself, is key. Believe in yourself, visualize it as a finished image, and it will happen. This is how all energy works, around and within you. You use your free will to influence the illusion around you. Have confidence in yourself, know yourself, and the world will be your oyster, so to speak. Have doubts and fears and you will falter, until you learn to pass these blocks. This is how you can use energy to your benefit. I will stress, as always, do not use these abilities to hurt others, including establishments, who make a living providing these services (gambling). You can use it, but do it more for fun. Generally, at least for myself, it back fires almost every time I use it to try to gain money with it.

When I play cards, and naturally most people around me, refuse to play cards with me, because I can see a lot of cards ahead of time, and can react appropriately. I don't do it intentionally anymore, but psycho-kinesis is so natural to me, that the cards just simply fall into place whenever I need them to. When I was younger, I tried, and used it, to understand the complete process of psycho-kinesis. Anymore, I do not intentionally influence cards or dice; they just automatically are drawn to me. You tell me the rules of the game, and those cards are drawn to me.

When you get excited or angry at cards, or the dice that was rolled, you will lose the ability to influence what you want, and you will just lose, and draw or roll, more of what you don't want. You must stay completely calm with no emotion or felt emotion. The calmer you are the better psycho-kinesis works. Cards and dice are the easiest illustration for explaining the idea of psycho-kinesis.

Psycho-kinesis can be used for anything around you, including the extremes of changing inanimate objects into forms which you desire. Most people won't be able to do this. Until you understand and experience this through oneness, you won't be able to consciously change objects.

The easiest way to help you understand psycho-kinesis in the third dimension is to think of it all as one big repeating, but progressive dream, as it is. Jesus knew this, and many hundreds before Jesus, and many others, since Jesus. Currently there are four, in the world, that possess this knowledge and understanding of what Jesus and others could do and mimic them, as others call miracles. They are what I would call "the potential to be". How I know there is four in the world is because I can feel them. They're energy levels are huge and stick out over everybody else like a beam of light shooting upwards outwards from everybody else's. The fourth was born 2 years before I wrote this book.

You can practice and imagine what you want to be in life. You can imagine making lots of money, having a big house, several cars, and etc. I've heard there are books out there in trying to harness this ability, and some could be correct. What they probably don't tell you is that you could be using your free will to force changes with energy. This you don't want to do, because there will be a price to pay for forcing will. I would prefer you to think of what you could do to help others, but this is your choice.

But for those of you, who would like to try it, these are the steps to achieve it. Each day spend a few minutes in meditation, imagining what you want, in your head. When you wake up in the morning repeat the image of what you desire and before you fall asleep, keep imagining that image of what you desire in your head. The more specific and detailed the image the better. It may take anywhere from a few days, to most of your lifetime, but it will happen. But, never give up trying. If you do, then your energy transfers elsewhere and you would have to start it up again, when you are ready to begin again.

Through psycho-kinesis, you are expressing your free will. Nothing in this world, or any other, can stop your free will, even karma. This is co-creation. When you have these images in your head, it is essential that you imagine them, as if; <u>you already have them or are them.</u> Don't think of them, as someday, I will have them. This can be hard to realize. Say you close your eyes, and hold these images, as such, and then the minute you open your eyes, you realize, you don't have them! This is only temporary. The physical takes a little time to work in the physical. That small delay. If you have doubts and fears in your mind about having what you want, you will slow it down tremendously, and it will never come to fruition because of your lack of faith in yourself. Have faith, not hope.

These are the keys, to psycho-kinesis. Confidence in yourself, no doubt or fear, and the realization that one's surroundings can and will change, to your free will. Psycho-kinesis, or use of your free will, can change anything in your life. You can always use it to enhance and unfold your soul. Use it, and see it opening your body up, and releasing your soul within you. This is the greatest gift you can give to yourself and to others.

Do not use it to influence or persuade others. You can and you will achieve it, if you follow my steps, but karma will come around if you use psycho-kinesis to influence or hurt others much faster to you upon doing this to others. The only thing I ever, intentionally influenced, for my own development, is where I see myself helping others, and, particularly, in healings of their soul's awakenings. I have used it intentionally for other stuff like money when I was younger, and I paid the price for it. Easy come - easy go.

If you get into arguments, say with your significant other, and you are insecure and very jealous, I say again, do <u>not</u> use this. Especially, if you feel you must be with them, and you can't live without them. First off, you need self-improvement, and confidence in yourself. Secondly, if you use these abilities to gain control over somebody else, you may get a strong lesson you'd rather not learn. Let's just say long-suffering will occur, until you decide to look within yourself, and get to know yourself. Then and only then, will you set yourself free. Not to mention, control through psycho-kinesis won't occur with strong emotions involved. There is nothing wrong with long-suffering, provided you learn from it. This can be very good for your spiritual awakening, increased compassion, and a better balanced understanding. The same holds true of those who hold positions of power over others. Be very careful in how you handle your power. Abuse it and you will lose it, eventually. Help others with it, and you will remain and prosper.

Psycho-kinesis works best, when you and the energy you are influencing, works together as one, and not forced by will. The great artists and musicians of our past, present, and future are truly using one form of psycho-kinesis. They see and/or hear the image in their mind, and can create it in the physical through the physical. Classic extreme examples of psycho-kinesis from the past that most of us have heard or read about are: Water to wine, walking on water, providing food for the masses, instant healings, etc. None of which, is difficult through understanding and awakening. It simply take's one thought, in oneness, to create such effects, in the physical.

One thing I have fun with is when I'm driving at night I usually use it to influence stop lights. I have done this during the day, but it tends to confuse drivers when they are expecting the lights to change as normal. So now I only stick to night time or during the day when there are less drivers around. I simply get calm and think of every light becoming or staying green as I'm approaching them. I see it even if it is currently red as I'm getting closer to it. I don't waver my speed much and just continue on as if it was green and 95% percent of the time it changes. Sometimes some drivers get smart in watching me cruising through traffic and all of the lights and start to follow my lead. If they get to far away from me they will hit a red light after I have gone through.

During the day and night with my intuition and kinesis I can see and feel where drivers around me are heading and when they will be turning soon. In doing this I can weave in out of traffic casually and just cruise through traffic. If I'm in a real hurry for some reason I have learned that I can influence drivers around and ahead of me. I can send them thoughts to move over into another lane which they do to give me a clear path.

This is simply one example of what you can use psycho-kinesis for. I use it almost daily. My family sees some of it, but most around me have no idea of what is going on around them. The possibilities of using psycho-kinesis is unlimited. Just remember, don't use it to harm others and don't use it to try to influence situations that you are judging and believing is correct with your own perception. I use it only in neutral situations and I don't use it very often when I know it will be too obvious to a lot of people. I'll show it to my kids as examples of what they could do, if they chose. Even my mom has watched me so so many times in using it. I can just see the thoughts in her head with it. She likes to play cards, so anytime we visit everybody knows we will be playing cards.

Energy/Tele-Kinesis

Tele-kinesis is one of my favorites, but I've found it to be, difficult let's say. Tele-kinesis is the ability of mind over matter to move objects, as they say, in definition. Yes, the mind is the physical creator, but telekinesis doesn't exactly quite work like this. That definition fits psycho-kinesis much better. I know through my experience of it. Tele-kinesis and psycho-kinesis are almost the same in nature. Tele-kinesis is simply the moving of objects, or anything, from one place to another. Without changing the structural integrity of the object, but just simply re-locating, or moving the object, through your thoughts alone. No physical touch is necessary or involved.

How to make this work first is your mind has to be in-tune with the vibrations around you much like a radio, to find this tuning. Let's say you concentrate on an item, like a drinking glass. Like psycho-kinesis, you must imagine that the drinking glass is moving towards you.

It is easier to imagine this with your eyes open. Just practice, and try not to force, but see and/or imagine that the drinking glass, and all of its energy, is cooperating with you, as one. Forced will, is slow and temporary. Cooperation is good and lasts, as long as, need be. In my opinion telekinesis is harder to achieve than psycho-kinesis because of this lack of force of will. Force of will with telekinesis really doesn't work. It's a blending in and with type of cooperation. Tele-kinesis works best if one cooperates with the object, almost as if they aren't even trying to make it happen. It just simply happens out of cooperation. Tele-kinesis is not spoon-bending. Spoon-bending is psycho-kinesis, and is much easier to achieve. You can bend a spoon with only your thoughts alone without ever touching the spoon. Most touch the spoon because it is easier to achieve this way because some of your energy rubs off sort of speak to help influence the desired effect and its easier psychological wise when an object is in front of you or in your hands to influence.

Healing/Physical/Mental/Origins Of

Healing. I hesitantly bring up healing, but I will describe healing in how to heal in any form and heal anything desired. I say, hesitantly, because all physical ailments are of an illusion and can be healed as such, or in the belief of the physical. It's more of a choice, between the two. Through energy or physical science. It's difficult to blend the two, except for instant healings. I prefer the illusion one, but the majority of society still lives in the world of the physical and prefers and understands the healing in this form much easier. I will discuss how to heal in both manners for you. I do both quite a bit to people, but usually they don't know what has happened. I've done it quite a bit, otherwise as well, when I have been asked to help.

Now with healing, you must first understand where illness and disease comes from. Granted, the medical community has causes of disease and illness, down to a pretty good science, except for a few, and there will always be the exceptions that medical science will always be trying to figure out. I will give hints to medical science in how to overcome this certain diseases and/or illness. These hints will eventually bring you to your exact answers. But it is always your choice.

Our bodies that we helped to create, in form and function, are basically perfect, except for the evolution of better enhanced development and/or hindrance thereof in our bodies. It's always our choice. We have had a lot of the later hindrance over the millenniums. In the beginning, we took our form and functions, more from the animals we observed, with some obvious changes. Our bodies, at least our mental and spiritual bodies, were much closer to our creator in oneness, to Him. We lived to be hundreds of years old; some lived to be millenniums old. Back then we chose more of when to leave our bodies, and when to return to our source. We have been doing this for millions of years. As science continues to progress they will keep finding humans being around a lot longer than they expected.

As we have evolved and progressively became more interested in experiencing, all of the physical surroundings around us, we have started to forget and neglect our connection to our one source of being. You could say we became selfish. We forgot where we came from or better yet, who we are and what we are capable of, in lieu of more material things. Once this evolution towards selfishness, greed and putting more emphasis on the material, was started, we found that we could no longer choose when to leave our bodies. As we went through these experiences, we became more self-indulgent into our being able to fix ourselves, and started to intentionally hurt, the physical bodies of others. Unfortunately, we forgot more and more about our oneness to our source, and became more and more absorbed into the physical, which I have stated earlier, is an illusion. This basically is the cause and effect, of illness and disease in us. Self created illness and disease.

As more and more time and evolution have passed, our disease and illnesses have changed and evolved, and became more complex as the nature of our physical minds have advanced into complexity. If you look back at history, which is limited to use as physical proof, you will always see a pattern of disease and illness. It has always been ahead of us, always evolving beyond what we can fix ourselves, even through medical science, and it always will be, except when turning back to our source, and trying to remember our true nature and source of being.

All disease and illness comes from our imaginations, which acts faster than we can fix physically. Every disease, illness, and accident can be traced back to cause. The cause is, generally found in previous lives from which we have once lived. Once again, karma! We have over-indulged, abused ourselves, whether mentally, spiritually, and/or physically, and then the most common – we hurt others. Remember; "Do unto others as you would have them do unto you." This was the start of disease, and its laws were set in motion.

The first and most obvious diseases started within our genes. Our genes could be timed, bring about certain conditions within our physical bodies, whether it was from birth to adulthood. Later on in our genes of adulthood, gives us the opportunity to gain wisdom, and understanding before the disease goes into effect. The disease/illness can be avoided, but it doesn't mean that it will be avoided.

The second is of our surroundings. In a lot of experiences, we need the same or similar surroundings, to duplicate the experience to learn from, but the surroundings can be completely different, to help the individual to experience it, in a different way, for understanding first, before the latter surroundings duplicate themselves. Remember, you are always given the opportunity to understand, first. That is grace.

Thirdly, the relationships surrounding you! The opportunities to bring you to understand, and forgive, thereby making amends in order to establish harmony, i.e., karmic release. In the beginning, we were still very close to our source, and had knowledge to reverse our situations. Now, we must take steps to remember to reverse our cycles. In not doing so, our world as a society, will continue to become worse in all conditions surrounding us.

To continue on, I say this hesitantly, because most people will have a very hard time understanding what I am about to say. Victims are needed to help others, in their experiences. In saying this, both the victim, and the victimizer, who needed to learn, by changing their roles, or perhaps one of them decided to help in the other's experience.

Please remember, that no one can hurt another, be it physically and/or mentally, without the other's permission, before they chose to return into this screenplay life. Our lives are like a movie. First, it is talked about with others, and then created like a screenplay when we come into physicality we then play it out like a movie. Keep in mind that you can change your life throughout with your free will for the better development of the soul or greater hindrance to the physical, your choice.

So look at it in this way. Somebody needs to be a victim, for another to experience and learn, from it, and nobody can hurt your physical body, without your permission. With permission I'm not taking about verbal or written permission. It's given from soul to soul ahead of time. Emotionally, I am like everybody else, I see murders and children crimes, and it gets to me, but I also realize and can see the reason behind it, in the macro view, as well, as each specific case. It's hard to live in two worlds of knowledge. I know how I should react in one way, and physically feel that way too, but then, I can see and feel the energy and karma patterns in motion from each specific case and understand the why. Life would be easier if I had no fore-knowledge of it, but with fore-knowledge I have developed true compassion, kindness, and forgiveness towards all, the victim and the victimizer.

Remember surroundings. Some surroundings have to be created similar because the victim needs these surroundings, to test themselves and see how they will react. Sometimes, I like the justice we have for some people, but I also understand that if they don't understand what they have done, deep within themselves, from what they have done, through understanding, that jail has been a waste of time, and they will come to understand, later on when their roles are reversed and they become the victims themselves. Another way to look at is if we didn't have jail, eventually they would run into the wrong person or group of people who would take them out for attempting to hurt them or others. We are still way behind karmically, and our primitive instincts are still in dire need of revision and correction. But, there is still and will always be instant karma.

So, hopefully, you now have, at least a partial understanding, of where disease and illnesses come from. You might ask, what about animals? They have almost the same diseases and illnesses as we do. Once we blended ourselves into physical matter, animals and plants became an extension of ourselves. We change ourselves, and animals themselves will change. Someday science will figure this one out. We crowd them, they crowd us. We are mean to each other, and they will be mean to us and of their own kind. Same applies to plants and trees.

Now there are several steps which you must figure out, before you can even heal yourself. If you follow these steps, and each step becomes completed, then karma, in this one aspect, will be released from you. From here, then you can heal yourself, from anything, as if, it never was a part of you i.e. you're being. This also includes healing anybody else, as long as each of the steps has been fulfilled. This is what most people call instantaneous healings, or so called – Like Jesus did. But, most of us cannot be healed instantaneously, because the steps haven't been fulfilled.

Remember, neither God nor we, can interfere with karma, except with our free will, which has more karma attached to it if we chose to use it for ourselves. Karma is our safety net – it is our i.e., our own justice system. No grace can be given from us to another, even Jesus. As long as karma is there, in the physical sense of an illness or disease, or whatever it is – it can only be soothed, as in pain killers – which only work for so long, or surgeries, which are only a temporary solution. This is why cancer, and other diseases can return, and generally more viciously, than before. They have to make up for the temporary loss of time you took. To change this through understanding, it will take changing your cell's vibrations, and the memory of your cells, changing, and then the cancer will be completely gone through your own body ridding of the disease or illness. Also, any current disease or illness you have, the severity of such, can also become lessened with spiritual awakening.

Oneness is the fastest and most efficient way to uncover your flaws, and through oneness, it will only allow you to take on as much as you can handle. But, let's say, you want to move-on, and you haven't achieved oneness yet, or don't want to. That's okay, oneness isn't for everybody yet. But, remember this, eventually all will have to achieve oneness to awaken spiritually. So why not try it now!

Take a look at your present surroundings, parents, and conflicts that you have had over and over again. The repeated ones are your biggest challenges to resolve. You must try to work on these. Usually, they will take several lifetimes to understand. Don't give in to them accept them as they just happen. Work on them.

Let's take an abusive relationship, for example. Psychology has figured out, to a degree, that who you are generally starts, in childhood with your parents, and your surroundings and they are correct in this interpretation. They can't prove reincarnation yet, but they are trying through hypnosis. Psychology can come very close to proving reincarnation if they continue on with this. The subconscious does have it all recorded for each individual. But, still beneath this, if the abuse continues on after you have become of legal age, and you can leave that situation, then that situation is up to you, to understand and deal with, accordingly. Some people get it early on, and never become like their parents; However, most become haunted by their abuse, and never learn to deal with its effects, and thus, become a mirror image of their previous abuse, and so it continues on, and passed down to their children.

First and foremost, the easiest way to understand this is try to understand the other person's surroundings, (This is why we are allowed to remember backwards, to reflect). Why were your parents the way they were? Why? Really dig deep. Once you find the root, then you can forgive, through understanding – You see? Everything is forgivable, and it is a lot easier to forgive when you have understanding of why it occurred. Then through your understanding and forgiveness, you will become forgiven yourself, and you will move-on, and seek the next level of better opportunities to experience, and you will be finished with that particular experience! This is how you release yourself from recurring situations in your life. You must understand, this is merely one example, of hundreds of thousands of examples, but they all have the same steps in healing the emotional, spiritual, and physical. Through understanding, you will learn forgiveness and kindness. This is one type of healing, you must understand, first. The majority of illnesses, you may experience will be of this type.

Healing/Genetically

The second type of healing is more of the genetically timed, or born with a handicap. This one is very common too. It practically goes hand-in-hand with those mentioned above. If you can release yourself from the first type of healing, the second type of healing can almost be dismissed. But, you could have karma from both, which most people do. The nice thing with the genetic one, is time is on your side for learning, before it reacts. If you learn from the first type or step of healing first, then the second category of healing is generally extended even longer for you, before your genes kick-in. Now with the second type of healing, let's just call it genetic healing, certain diseases, such as cancer, heart disease, and every other kind of illness comes from several other things.

First, your surroundings. Second, let's say, for example, you have physically abused others in another life, in such a manner, that you have crippled them for life. If you have not come into understanding, of such, then diseases of the nervous system generally make themselves apparent, later on – such as, multiple sclerosis. Multiple sclerosis and every illness, or disease is reversible through understanding. Let's say, you have judged others so harshly you injured them physically, but you did not cause their death. You will suffer diseases, through your glandular system i.e., - diabetes and some cancers. Most other diseases, such as, heart disease and most cancers, virus, cold and etc if not directly connected to your glands, or nervous system, are simply caused through your own environment and choices you have made. Your own indulgences of the physical, and perhaps from your own fears, that you have chosen to ignore and put off.

Generally, most people will have a combination of, two to three of these diseases, or illnesses, within their lifetime. These are the causes and the answers to them, which will change permanently, unlike the temporary solutions to them, of medical science. You see, medical science tries really hard to cure you in any manner required, but they can only do so much. If you want to rid yourself of disease and illness, you must first start with yourself. Doctors can only see as much as a mechanic can with a car. They will probably miss the underlying cause, because they can't see it. Even with all of their machines, the answer is still up to you. I hope you understand this! You, and only you, can change and pioneer your destiny. Remember, we have to pass on. But, you can choose when, and what form, when you do pass-on, rather than letting fear rule your surroundings.

Self-Healing

Once you have fully digested what I have told you from the above chapter, I'm going to show you, how you can heal yourself, and then heal others. It can be from instant healing, to years of healing needed, to heal yourself fully. It's all up to you. Remember, your mind is the physical creator and can beat anything – that's the beauty, of free will and grace through understanding and forgiveness. Free will can change everything for you, and it is given to us, to do so, as co-creators. If you release yourself from your burdens, then you have a new choice, and a new life to decide on, what to do from there. Free will and grace gives you that opportunity. If you want to force options against karma, which you can temporarily, then your free will can. Remember, you are a co-creator. This means that you are capable of anything that God Himself can do, and I'm not kidding, nor joking about this. It is true fact! If you could remember your past, in the very beginning, as I have, you would be amazed about what you, did, and we're capable of doing. Then you could look at yourself currently and kinda of be like what the hell have I done to myself.

Okay, let's say the doctors have found a tumor, or cancer within your body. First, try to understand your situation. Why has this situation come to you? Indulgences, perhaps? Second, you must release judgments of the cancer. It is what it is and now it's time to deal with it. Try to understand why you have the cancer, for instance. Overindulgences, genetic? Third, healing is ready to begin for you.

Let's say, the doctor takes an X-ray or CT scan. Ask to see the X-ray. From this, you will come across the origin of the cancer in your body. From here, hopefully, you have practiced on becoming sensitive to your own body. Through imagery, you can move your blood flow around within your body, and can activate certain glands and organs, to boost your immunity levels. I realize this is easier said, than done. But, with practice, you can. I know, and I have done it myself. Seeing this in others, I can see how it all works. I have used a lot of different methods in healing others, and through this, I have come to understand, and see how it all works. Remember, your mind has incredible power, when you put it to use. Just use it, and your physical body will respond to it. Think of you as a driver of your vehicle. You control your vehicle. Do you crash it, speed it all of the time, or take care of your vehicle. You control it for the most part.

You must understand that I am not a doctor, nor pretend to be one. If you have any doubts, please ask your physician. If your doctor is closed-minded, then ask others. They all have different experiences and opinions. Through the use of imagery, let's say, you have a tumor in your breast, which indicates abuse to others. I thought I would mention this one since it has become so public.

Get into a relaxed position, and calm your body and mind. Then, imagine that you are inside your body looking at the tumor you saw in your X-ray. Look at it all around in a 360 degree or 3D. Eventually, you will be able to see how and where the tumor is attached, in your mind. Your mind will receive pictures of the tumor. From here, you can now start to see your heart speeding up a little bit, but not too much. Be patient! It doesn't take much speeding up to heal yourself. Just a short walk could duplicate the speed you would need. Visualize your brain sending impulses, or signals shooting down your nerves to your heart, then your lungs will kick-in a little bit more, for increased oxygen. See it. Become it.

Once you have done this, the rest is fairly easy. Now go back and visualize that tumor in your breast again. Simply by going back to the image, your body will start to send extra blood flowing in that direction, and increase your immunity levels, to target this area, specifically. Your body feels what your mind is trying to do. But, we are not going to just depend upon your body; we are going to influence it and push it. When you see that tumor again, imagine your glands and bones producing or pumping out little white cups, you can use your imagery, just building-up, and then they start to move with your blood, into the affected area of the tumor.

Once these little cups get there, see them attacking that tumor. Just pounding it, and trying to take it apart, and scoop it away. As pieces come off the tumor, imagine those little cups are cruising through your bloodstream, reaching your liver and to your kidneys, and then exiting your body, or going into your bladder. Afterwards, you should have urgings to release your toxins, in wanting to use the restroom. Taking water before and afterwards helps your body perform that much better.

The more you practice this, the better you will become at this, and your body will automatically start to attack the cancer, without much effort on your part. After awhile, your body will come to recognize the tumor as a foreign body, and will attack it, on its own. If you wish to test this to make sure you are actually achieving it, take a quick break from your imagery, and put your hand over the affected area. That area should be hotter, than any other area on you. If you have a mirror, you might be able to see that area getting more flush, than other surrounding areas from the blood flow and healing. If you test this, and it is hotter, you are healing yourself. Like I said, it may take a few days to months of doing this, once or twice a day, for about ten minutes or so, depending upon the damage caused. But, this does work, and will work. If the doctor wants to get you into surgery right away or soon, please do. You don't want to take too long with cancer. Some you have years and others months to a year depending on what you have plus it probably has already been in your body for years growing before you realized it.

I am opposed to chemo, because it destroys your good cells of memory. By destroying them, you can actually create more cancer, as time goes by. The method I presented to you does work, and will start to work right away. Again, I am not a doctor, nor do I pretend to be one. If you want chemo and your physician tells you that you need it. Then this is your call and you might head what the doctor has told you. I will never tell you to ignore what a physician has prescribed. I am not there and I don't see what you have while the doctor is there and present at the time.

This method can also be used to reverse aging of the skin, lose weight, and obviously, reactivate your immune system. I have done this, and this is why my body is normally hotter than most. I have just turned up my healing abilities, because of the way I eat, certain indulgences and beat up my body with the work I do. With eating, you must get rid of the toxins daily, if not more. If you don't, then your system is letting all of these preservatives, and fat, sit in your body, and become a nuisance or added stress to your body.

Following these above steps, there shouldn't be anybody who will be overweight, unless they have another cause. Following these same methods you can increase your immune system which will burn your excesses off naturally. Gland issues are a little bit trickier, but can still be reversed, even diabetes. They come directly from the soul. Much learning and understanding is a must, before the disease can be reversed. Cancer and heart disease can be easier to reverse, than certain gland problems. With diabetes, work on increasing your immune system first, before you try to start to reactivate certain glands. Do this and then get a picture of the gland or glands where the problem are originating from your doctor and then with imagery you can move blood flow temporarily to the glands to try to jump start the gland(s). This could take days to weeks, months or years to reactivate the gland(s). But, make sure you understand the underlying causes first. Yes, I know it sounds extremely simple, but it is that easy.

Let's talk about obesity here. It seems to be so popular anymore, so let's break it down for the all natural way to end it. Obesity is actually very easy to fix. The main problem from it is preoccupation and self confidence. The easiest way, excluding, oneness, and walking, which is excellent for you, is simply, to speed up your metabolism. Speeding up one's metabolism would cure a lot of disease and illness's on its own. In meditation and as you fall asleep at night you simply imagine what you want to look like, each day when you wake up in the morning and before you go to bed at night. This is a two part healing for you to speed it up for yourself. From here, concentrate on your body's blood, circulating throughout your body, and grabbing pieces of fat, and carrying them away.

Circulation is also a main key to reversing the aging process. Positive thoughts keep your blood flowing, while negative or depressing thoughts slow your circulation and metabolism down. If you enjoy being overweight this is your choice, and it's perfectly okay to be so. I'm not here to tell you otherwise.

You see, first you must understand with obesity; which medical science knows too, is that we have evolved quite fast, within the last one hundred years, with technology paving the way. Much faster, then our physical bodies could adapt, and/or evolve. Eventually, our bodies will catch up. Our physical bodies are used to being active and in motion. However, our bodies now are much less active, than they used to be. So exercise is needed for a few more generations, until evolution catches up. But, excess food will still create, excess fat. Eventually, through evolution our bodies will become less dependent on food, and our cravings will lessen.

If you choose to increase this method of self-healing, you simply add good old neutral energy to your body. As I mentioned in early paragraphs, remember the part I mentioned on absorbing energy, through your hands. Before you start imagining the process of speeding up your heart, concentrate first, with absorbing energy through your hands. In a relaxed position, put your hands outward from your body (if you like); hold your palms upwards toward the ceiling or sky. Once relaxed, imagine invisible or just energy of any color pouring into your hands. Or think of your hands as a vacuum, just sucking the air or energy. See the energy in your mind, pouring into your hands, and then traveling down your arms, and into your stomach area. Or the energy can shoot from your hands, and be directed towards your stomach area. You must imagine this, and it will happen. Whenever I am contemplating on absorbing energy, it automatically starts to pour into my hands. If I turn my hands upwards, the energy immensely jumps, to pour in more energy. Proof of this, is when your hands become hot, as well as your stomach area. From here, just let your stomach area distribute the energy to where it chooses.

Now you can go into seeing your blood flow, and your heart pump through visualization. You should feel much more energized, in the beginning of this, than when you absorb energy at first. You can also absorb energy, anytime during the day or night, to increase your energy levels, and keep you more relaxed and concentrated, on the task at hand. Self-healing is really that simple, just practice and patience. You are just a giant battery. Never give up and have confidence in yourself. You can do it! Everybody can do it! Just rid yourself of your skepticism, doubts, and fears.

Healing of Others/Introduction

Healing of others. When you heal others completely, or instantly within seconds, the disease or illness are banished, because all karmic conditions have been met. This is rare, but far from impossible. It actually happens a lot. A lot of obstacles must be cleansed, beforehand. Jesus would have healed more people instantly, if other conditions had been met. The good thing is that you can see these conditions in others through oneness. It is actually easier to heal someone who was born with an illness, such as being blind, than one brought on, later in life. Remember, lessons learned. If you have a difficult time with this, (most will initially), don't give up. Just accept it, as if you are trying to help another. Action is very powerful. If they are ready for, instant healing, timed healing, or simply, temporary healing, your action could be all that is required to heal them.

Before, I heal anybody I look at the person or talk to them and see their conditions. This is a hard one to describe because I can look at anybody and see the patterns of energy flowing, breaks, restrictions and conditions that have brought this on. So how I get you to see the same thing I'm not sure. Practice the meditation, practice healing, practice using your intuition until you get there. You might achieve one day and you might not ever.

Also, something that I do before I even heal somebody. Is like the 12 year old ghost came to me and I couldn't answer her questions then boom all the information came to me. I hit that vibrational link before, I even attempt to heal anybody. Then I get this same type of information comes to me about them almost instantly. I will know if I can even heal them or not. I will know how much I can help or heal them. Maybe it will only be a temporarily healing that will only last for so long. Maybe I can only relieve some of the pain they are in or in some cases, I realize there is nothing I can do for them. What they have is brought on completely by themselves. This I cannot fix. It's completely on them to decide and fix on their own. They set it up this way. So even if I try to heal them it could simply speed up there disease or illness. It's a built in safety measure for themselves. If you try it it will only make it worse. Each of the cases, I will tell them or whoever has contacted me to help them. I will tell them what I can or can not do for them. I will tell them what to expect from the healing and how it should go. How long it will last or be fixed for good.

Once I see them, then I can see their energy patterns, within their body, moving around. I have never seen one pattern of energy be exactly the same in another. Close, but it is always a little bit different, as in, everybody is different, in some way. Such as, fingerprints or one's DNA. It is never the same. They could have exactly the same condition, but two completely different ways of healing them.

Now I have to express this, so everybody understands this. When a doctor heals or fix's you, replaces an organ or whatnot, it is simply fixing an energy break as i see it. Just as when I heal somebody, I am not healing them! I am simply giving their body the energy needed to heal itself. Yes, I can direct the energy towards the breaks and try to bypass them, but it's your own body that can fix the energy disruption ultimately. Our bodies are perfect rebuilding structures. We built them this way.

When a doctor fix's you they are usually only fixing your energy disruption temporarily even though they look at it as a physical problem or disruption. Sometimes, your body will accept it as its own and the energy disruption is fixed permanently. Eventually, far from now science will view the body as a electrical machine vs a physical one. Remember, physical is the end result!

Now, let's make this perfectly clear. You can heal anything. I've healed plants, cats, dogs (even with broken bones), and various other animals. They are actually very easy to heal, because their energy is neutral. I've healed, so many people, whether it is mental and/or physical, through touch, or using my mind on so many different things. As I have advanced in my awakening I have learned that I can heal others simply by looking at them or even using a picture, when I chose to do so or even in my sleep. I've awoken and healed the elderly on their death beds, to give them some more time, to say their goodbye's, and get their things in order, and I've healed others without a physical body (a passed on soul), but this is a different subject. I have sometimes, even crossed-over when somebody has passed-on, and walked with them, until their bright light has shown the way for them.

Healing of Plants and Animals

Let's talk about plants and animals, first. They're easier for you to understand, at first. Plants and animals are very neutral in their energy, meaning they don't have the will nor the desire (ego) to try to force and move energy around. They just simply do their thing, and domestic animals generally are only trying to serve and love (companionship). Animals, plants, and especially domestic animals, are extensions of our own selves, and of our surroundings. They are more like the Earth than to us. We can abuse them, and they will adapt, and will suffer our own diseases and illness, of such, to try to help us have compassion, kindness, patience and love for one another. They are all very precious to us, and the Earth. To heal them, it is very easy, and a good start for beginners.

Let's start with plants, trees, and flowers. Healing works more efficiently, if you can see their energy flow, with your own physical eyes, or within your head. Through oneness you can. If not, just use your imagination. Their energy comes in from the ground, water and air, more from their roots. It flows by spreading throughout each branch and leaf, while moving upwards to the top, and then exits the same way it came in from its roots. You can see energy exiting in smaller amounts, from their leaves. This is their aura. It looks more like small amounts of mist rising out of them.

To help plants, trees, or flowers, there are two ways of doing such, and the changes usually take one or more days, to react too healing. Trees and plants are patient. One is with imagery; absorb energy into your body. Once you fill up with energy, imagine then your energy flowing back out through your hands, into the plants. Your energy will actually swirl around the plants/trees energy, initially, before starting to seep into their root system. If you can see their energy patterns, you will be able to see the normal energy flow of the plant now growing much larger and brighter, so to speak, and you'll see the plant's absorption abilities increase. Plants react to the surrounding energy around them. I've taken absolutely dried-up dead plants, and brought them back to growing again, the next day, just through energy. Some, within hours.

The second way of healing plant's, is simply by keeping your own energy vibration higher. Just by simply trying to know yourself, and increasing your spiritual awakening, plants, flowers, and trees will just start to grow better around you. Positive thoughts versus negative thoughts, as well. Remember, some people are called to have green thumbs. This is one way to figure out where you are spiritually. I don't treat my plants as good as I should, with watering, soil, and sunlight. But, everybody around me knows that plants, trees, and everything else just grows around me like crazy. Whether they have poor soil, no soil, or water, they just grow. But, I must be around. If I am gone for too long, the plants will start to shrink and diminish. That's basically it; plants are just like elements or essentials of life. They respond to music, companionship, and energy.

Now, onto wild and domestic animals. Wild animals will react as we do to them. They are driven primitively, but drawn to society, as a whole. They react to us, as we treat them. If it is peaceful around them, they act accordingly. If they are suppressed, and hunted, they will act accordingly, around us, as well as, to their own kind. We have much to understand of our thoughts and actions, and may never fully discover our own relationships to animals, and the earth. What we create as a society, our surroundings will mimic.

One interjection I will mention here, which most won't consider to be a negative and it applies to all. Anytime I know I will be able to heal somebody I give them a warning. If I heal you I am also changing your life span. It will increase and usually I don't know by how much. Just a by product of it I have noticed. Anytime you heal an animal, for the most part, their life span will also increase. I have had, and been around pets, that were supposed to be crippled and die soon, and instead I and many others have witnessed them, live a lot longer, than what their average life spans were even supposed to be and still alive decades later, and witnessed their release of their injury or illness. I have only come across two animals that I have been unable to heal, and it was simply because, it was their time. I have comforted them, and released them from most of their pains. Again, like the movie "Green Mile" I saw at the ending of it and was like how did they come up with that? Because that's what mine does too with the life extension.

You can see healing in animals much more rapidly. Generally, if it works in the first place, you will notice a big difference, immediately, when the healing is done. Sometimes, it happens instantly to several minutes to a few days to get it out of their system, completely. But, with animals and plants, I generally make direct contact, with my hands-on them. With people I look at their surroundings, before I touch them, in a healing manner, which can be from just slightly above to actually reaching out, and touching their affected area(s) or just holding their hand. I've learned my touch can be a little shocking and hot to them.

Now, just like plants, I can see energy patterns in the animals body, and I can then absorb energy, and touch their affected area, and usually around their affected area. I help release all, or the partial amounts, of their pain. Animals intuitively know what I am going to do, and generally, they become very submissive and calm for me. Sometimes afterwards, I have had them take off running from me like they were puppies again; to turning around, and cuddling with me, or just looking at me, while they walk off. I can see what animals are thinking, within their eyes, just as we feel we can see things in each others, eyes. However, our eyes are much deeper with thought, than that of animals, which are much thinner, almost surface-like. Their thoughts are more of feelings...They don't have thoughts like ours. Remember, they are primitively driven. Any healing I do of animals, plants, or people, I know they always feel my increased heat or energy, generated within their affected areas, or throughout their bodies.

I really enjoy helping nature and animals with healings because of their innocence of being healed either way. They simply do what they must do one way or another without judgment. I highly recommend trying to heal plants and nature in general first. If successful, which anybody can do, you will see the results of it within days. Being neutral they react quite fast to energy or healings.

Healing of Others

Now on to people. There are several ways to heal. Direct contact (which I rarely do). Healing with your hands above certain parts of another's body. Healing from our thoughts (as in prayer) and intentional thought healing. Healing can be anything, from spiritual to the mental, and to the physical. I prefer spiritual, because from spiritual, all healing can be achieved. We'll go into the physical, first.

You see, healing others begins with your, motives, first. You must be neutral in your thinking while going into the healing. If you are emotionally tied to the person, it will be much much harder to achieve. Your motives must only be to help the person you are going to heal with no thought of a return of money or something back to yourself. Prayer is a good start, for purifying you're, motives, until you get the mindset down to carry this mindset to help others.

Before, I heal, anybody, I look at the person to see their flow within their body. Then, I see where the breaks, restrictions, and blocks are in their energy flow. From there, I then pick up the true causes of the problem. I can see if they are ready to be healed, or see whether the injury, disease, or illness, stems from another past life, and what they did to incur it, or if it was incurred in this life.

You see, no matter whom you are, you will not be allowed to heal another person, unless they agree to seek their healing i.e., agreeing to being healed by you or another. From here, if I am allowed, healing can happen instantaneously, or take a few minutes, several days, or possibly weeks to months to fully heal. In my mind, I then see where I need to set my hands, and/or surrounding areas. My hands are usually above the person. I very rarely make contact. I only make contact on a person, if I am going to intentionally send a shock of energy to their soul, or I feel that their healing needs a direct jolt, of energy, to get their body's energy re-aligned; especially, in mental disorders. Sometimes, I will heal others through a simple holding of their hands and then send them energy this way. It's more comforting to them. Others I have already talked to their soul, so to speak, with a glance and then when I hold their hand(s) I will send them healing energy without them being conscious of what I am doing for them. I've done this a lot in hospitals for others.

I've extended the lives of many elderly through direct contact to their hands to help them become more conscious, and therefore, enabling them to say they're goodbye's to their family members. When an individual's time is near, I am only able to extend their lives, temporarily, and relieve some of their pain and suffering. Each individual I have healed, in this manner, generally averages, around three days of time. A couple of them gained almost two weeks of time.

I will add this experience for others. This I did decades after I wrote this book, but a good example of how it works for me. My mom collapsed one day at work and was taken to the hospital by an ambulance. My dad and sister arrived at the hospital before me. When I arrived, I told my mom the usual greetings, love you and how you doing type of thing. She looks at me and says do you know what's wrong. I said, I do. She said, can you help me? Yes, I can, but if I do you will get extended and I don't know how long that will be. She said, sounds good to me while chuckling a little bit in laughter.

Deep down within me I know I can heal her, but I also realize at the same time this is my mom. One of the biggest emotional bonds I can have with somebody. So I'm honestly thinking to myself I'm not sure how well this is going to work because of the bond.

So I take a deep breath and say ok. I told her when the doctors come back this is what they are going to tell you and what they think it is. They will re-test and run a couple of more tests on you and then release you in a few hours after discovering you are perfectly fine now kinda of scratching there heads like what just happened? So I grabbed her hand and put my other hand on top of hers and just held it for a minute or so. Then I looked up at her and said, ok it's done. Then soon after the doctor came in and nearly repeated almost everything I told her they would say to her. They wanted to run some more tests and this is what they think it is and etc. So I said my goodbye and said I will come by your house tonight and see you and we can play some cards if you like.

She was released within a few hours later from the hospital and walked out as if nothing had ever happened to her. I don't remember what I told her the doctors were going to say or what she even had. I do this stuff so much that I just can't keep track of everything. Plus this information I get can vanish from my memory because my conscious mind hasn't memorized it. It's more like outside information that comes in and then disappears. Like a person who is a channel. Maybe because it hasn't run directly through my memory it just isn't absorbed into it. I don't know. The same applies to anybody I have given information too in questions they have asked me. I just can't seem to recall the information the same as I can a memory of my own.

Just remember, anybody can heal anything. Trust me, when my son was seven years old, he healed his mother instantly for the first time, completely on his own through caring and compassion. He didn't even realize what he had done, until I sat down and explained it to him. He is an extremely giving and caring soul. Everyone has known this for most of his life. He is always surprising us with his caring and compassion for others. He has the gift of tuning into others.

At this point, imagine neutral energy around you starting to pour into your body through your hands and going into your abdomen area. From here, set your hands above the affected area and/or surrounding areas of where you feel that your hands need to be. Not all of the time is your hand or hands, going to be over the affected area, because if it's not the cause; the affected area is simply, an effect, of the cause. Then, imagine the energy coming into your body and pouring into their body, over the affected areas.

If you can get absorbing energy down, you can feel your own body filling up with immense amounts of energy, so when you pour it into another, that person's body, in those areas, will begin to heat up, and could even become hot to the touch, or warmer. If their affected areas are warming up, at least, to a degree, you are starting to affect their healing capacities. If you can see the energy flow within their bodies, you will, visually see, the energy in their body flowing with large amounts of energy in those areas, and see their energy trying to re-align, and correct itself, like a broken or severed nerve(Yes the body can rebuild a nerve). From there, the healing can be nearly instantaneous to taking days to weeks, for the energy to re-align itself, and fix the physical problem. Have them drink a glass of water before and after the healing. It does help the body with removing toxins.

How long should one heal for? This varies for each individual. In the beginning, only try to heal another for one to five minutes. Yes, true healings are very brief in time. Anything past this would be very draining for both involved. So try your best for one to five minutes with your hands and let it go. Wait one to three days later and try it again. Talk with the other and see if any effects have started to occur or if they are feeling better in any way? Usually they will be feeling better in some way. If not, don't worry or give up. Keep trying. With action and patience it does work. I will never tell you to try to do something, knowing that it won't work. These methods will work and are over many many millions of years old in their origins. With my own healings for others, over time my healings have gained in speed and efficiency, which yours will too. My average healings are around five to twenty seconds. Many are much faster within one or two seconds and some up to one minute or so.

I understand most people might not see these energy patterns of others, and this is okay. It takes a lot of practice, but oneness will help you, tremendously. Even if you can't feel the energy pouring into your body, don't worry about that, it comes with time and practice. As long as your mind is set, and your motives are of the highest, to help another, try it. Even if it works a little bit, that is perfectly okay. You can probably help relieve them of some of their pain, temporarily. With some people, you will simply reduce their blocks or restrictions, within them so that their own bodies can naturally start to reverse the problem.

Now always remember, that *YOU* are not the one healing them. You can never heal another without their permission. You can only help them. Any healings achieved are done from the person being in agreement with the healing – within themselves. You are only helping with your own energy, and positive action, towards them. It's up to them to accept, and heal. Even in instantaneous healings, they must accept, and have all conditions met. If they are met and in agreement, your energy combines with theirs and their soul awakens to a degree and the healing is instant. Remember, everything is an illusion that seems to be real to us.

When I talk about permission, it can be through them physically, saying yes, or (what I do most of the time) to get the answer from their soul. I've only had two people ever tell me no to a healing, most people, at least, figure what do they have to lose by you trying. If a person is unconscious then I can simply ask their soul obviously.

Sometimes, it is possible to pull some of the energy from the other person into your energy. By doing so, you will start to experience some of their symptoms, emotions and feelings that they are feeling. If that happens, don't worry, but after the healing which should last no longer than ten minutes, or less at a time, concentrate on absorbing more energy into your own body, and imagine your body flushing the energy through you, to re-gain your emotional connection back to yourself. You can inherit or gain their illness and/or disease, in the emotional connection and can be felt by the combining of the two energies, as if you have what they have. It is only an emotional bond, so don't worry. The best way to make sure you don't emotionally bond, is to only imagine your energy going into the individual, and when you are done pouring energy into them, immediately pull your hands away. Your hands are very sensitive to reception. The more calm and neutral you keep your emotions going into a healing, the less chance you have of their energy and emotions transferring into you. That's why calmness and intent are very important. The more emotionally detached you are from the individual, you are trying to heal the more efficient your energy will be. But, always be kind and compassionate.

A second way to heal is through simple prayer let's call it. When you pray for somebody, do so once again with only the highest of motives – which is always of helping them (Which most healers do when they pray for somebody). To enhance prayer, when you are praying for somebody, let's say with an injury, while praying for them, imagine what the person looks like, and then imagine good things, or good energy flowing from yourself to them. You see when individuals pray to God, they are actually attracting energy to themselves. This is why, when individuals pray they can begin to feel inspired. I will say again, that God is of neutral, non-judging energy. What you choose to do with the energy is up to you. Remember, God does not judge others, we only judge ourselves. Prayer does help in this manner. It has to be directed towards the person in need and not so much to God. When people use prayer to God in that way to help others it's kinda of like trying to make God the middleman. It's much more effective and efficient to direct your prayers to the actual person in need. Think of God as being the neutral energy that you are pushing out to the person in need. The reason I know this is because I can see the energy involved when others pray and watch what it does. You are a lot more effective when it goes directly to them.

The third manner, (which I do quite a bit), without others realizing, is like praying, but I would prefer to call it, intentional healing. It's the same as praying, except instead of praying to God directly, and receiving energy in this manner, and then hopefully putting it back out to the one, you are praying about, I absorb or use the energy I have within myself, and direct it towards the individual(s) directly. No hands or anything is used, except my thoughts. When I do this, I can see their energy flow patterns, and see the circumstances involved, and then send energy their way. I rarely instantly heal individuals, because of the circumstances that they must come to understand, for themselves. But, I can and do send a lot of helpful healings to individuals. After a lot of practice, I have found this method much more efficient than being in the presence of somebody and using my hands on them. Or I can look into their eyes even with a glimpse and send them some energy to help them physically.

Sometimes I will send energy with positive thoughts to help inspire people, when they are thinking of positive developments that they feel are major goals they want or are contemplating, and wish to achieve. I call it more of a push, or surge of energy, to help encourage their development. Many times, I will send energy thoughts to individuals who are feeling down, or are trying to figure out the ways of the world. I can send others thoughts of answers to help inspire them, and help them in their spiritual journey to awakening.

I have often healed so many people this way. Just hanging out in a line at a store and as I'm just standing there I can see there energy flows and etc so I can just send them energy to them without them even knowing what is going on. Sometimes, their energy jumps and they start feeling really good in line or start standing more erect and confident all of a sudden. Or become very talkative and how they feel so good right now for no reason or hurt less.

I actually prefer this supportive healing over instantaneous physical healings. Physical healings are only healings of the physical, which in all actuality, are the least of my concerns. Your spirituality i.e. spiritual growth is so much more important to me. I would prefer to erase karma and awaken their spirituality for individuals, then heal them physically. You see, when you reach understanding and patience, your physical body will change, automatically, because your physicality is the effect of – the end result, of your changed thinking. What you think, you experience.

Don't feel that you must be in the presence of the individuals to heal them. Like I have mentioned earlier, all I need is a simple picture of an individual. Just seeing that picture of them, I can do anything, if conditions are met. I know exactly what needs to be healed, their manner of being, manner of psychology, their strengths and weaknesses, their soul, if they are alive, or passed-on, etc.

If you are aware of the vibrational link that I talk about, anyone can contact you on it and vice versa. No pictures or anything needed, except the trying of contact. It would be the same as praying to God. You don't know who God is, but you are sending a vibrational link of need to Him. You just need to realize God's vibrational link is in everything everywhere. No need to look up to the sky or heaven for Him. Just simply talk.

I would recommend trying this method and see where your results go. It could be more efficient result wise for you. Remember that vibrational link.

Judgmental Thinking/Labels

Now let's talk about some subjects that are very dear to me and the basis of this book. You must understand, I see and feel, what I am going to talk about, all over the world, everyday, and we must change it - The judgment of others. I'm going to talk about, labels – judgmental thinking of others, reversal of judgments, fears, reversal of fears, weight control, personal appearance, money, power, greed, fear, economic status, doubts, jealousy, relationships, and wars.

Labels and judging of others just drive me crazy, its everywhere and is the biggest gargantuan thing that I see, within people., besides fear. It's absolutely ferocious. If you could see into others thoughts, as I do every day, the ugliness of what people really think, is overwhelmingly horrible and ridiculous. The saddest part is that most of it is directed towards one another. Most of us as a society, would like to see crime, greed, doubts, fears, jealousy and anger of all kinds reduced in our world.

This one thing, the judgment of others, would dramatically change our world unlike any other thing or action, or constructive energy that we could do, for our preservation and peace. (Most of us wouldn't even recognize our society anymore, compared to the present). Our governments would be miniscule, tax's would be so minimal, crime would almost be non-existent, reduced jails and law enforcement, wars could become obsolete, very little need for rules, or directing for daily living, HOA's and exclusive clubs would become extinct – We would have a lot more freedom and able to have more experiences of spiritual awakening. We wouldn't need to be controlled, for our own safety. Could you imagine this?

Helping others with positive thoughts towards each other, would become the common daily ritual. Don't get me wrong, there is always others helping others and having good positive thoughts. This is always refreshingly good and comforting to see. I salute all who do this daily!

Ask yourself, "Why do we judge others?" Is it over fear of others? Others have accumulated more than you? Others look better than you, physically? Do others wear different clothes than you? Is their hair nicer or different than yours? Or do they wear suits, or clothes with holes in them? Do they have a nice car, or an older car? Do they appear to be more intelligent or below average? Do they go to Church, or not? Are they professional, such as lawyers and doctors, or are they construction or garbage men? Are they of a different color skin? Do they appear to be on drugs, alcohol, or do they steal, lie, and cheat? Are they married, or not? Do they like the same gender, or not? Have you ever asked yourself, why do I have these thoughts? Really have you ever thought about, the thoughts you have and why?

I see this daily in people within their thoughts think the following: If it hasn't become so second nature to them: Since nobody can see my thoughts, except God, then it's okay to have these thoughts because I'm not saying them out loud to others. If you have nothing nice to say, then don't say anything! This is where I see us going wrong. Your thoughts will create your surroundings. So, if your thoughts are always judging others, then your thoughts bring you even more opportunities to judge others, and create more continuous patterns in your surroundings to judge others.

You see, if your thoughts are more positive towards others, your surroundings will change dramatically for the positive. Other people with positive thoughts start to become attracted to you. Like – attracts like, in judgments. How important, here it is to see – Your judgments of others have shaped your character whether you realize it or not.

We begin to learn judgments of others, from just before our birth to throughout our lives. We are taught a lot from our surroundings, initially, and our parents, and associates. We must understand that our initial surroundings are given to us, to understand experience and learn from, or choose not to accept. These are opportunities given to us, by our choices of what we need to experience again, or help others in what they need, to experience and understand.

We initially judge, to survive. After we have learned how to survive, we then learn further judgments, from our parents, religions, schools, and others within our environment. From here, it is up to us to decide for ourselves, which, we are going to accept, or refuse. Eventually, we must turn back, and release ourselves, of all judgments of others, to become, truly free. I see few doing this, while the majority get progressively intertwined into the physicality and drama of life.

When I was young, around the age of twelve, I started to notice these judgments of others, especially in religion, and that's why I began to question, and started to notice judgments towards others, by looking around at various religions. They would say one thing, and then say the Bible says, this and that, and then they would almost always do the opposite. Don't get me wrong, there have always been those you have tried their best to practice what they teach and I always give them my credit for trying to do their best with what they have.

From here, I started to notice the same with racism. I'd hear people say they don't judge others by the color of their skin, but then, they would treat them differently, on every occasion. I found the same instances true in politics (over the different parties), government, business, most religions, general public, etc.

As I got older 24, I tried to help teach in supposedly a more open or non-denominational religions, and there they still practically always, made the same, judgments and prejudices. I was told that I was not allowed to teach others, until I learned their beliefs and only taught their teachings. I tried other houses of worship and always the same thing. Granted they saw me as a very young person that they didn't quite understand where I was coming from, at that time, and probably would still hold true today, and yet that, hit me as a prejudice, against the young and supposedly, uneducated in spiritual matters and training. Why does it have to be in their manner of teaching? Can you not progress as science and technology progress's? Don't become held to the past and supposedly be able to serve the future unfoldment.

At this point, is when I realized, that in my future to be, it is better for myself that I do not join any organized religious organization, per se, because of any future influence I might have on their particular teachings. Soon after that, I have always known what my future was going to entail. It was simply going to be a matter of being up to me as to when I should decide and accept what my future would be.

Once again, let me emphatically state how important to humanity, as a whole, and critical to our spiritual awakening to start to reverse these tendencies towards judgment of others. The best and most efficient way, is through understanding and patience. For example, say you see somebody with different skin color. What runs through your mind? They are uneducated, dressed differently, act differently and possibly they steal and/or lie? Do they really? When you catch these thoughts going through your mind, ask yourself, are these thoughts based on my experience or society's shortcomings? If they are society-based, there is a very good chance, they are wrong. If they are experience-based, when and where did I first encounter them? Was it an opportunity for me to be kind to another and non-judgmental, which I missed by doing the opposite or being neutral?

You must understand you attract what you fear, and fear nullifies any positive opportunities to release, previous judgments. Understand you cannot judge others, as a generality. Everybody is different, to a degree. They have their own karma and their own opportunities to experience and decide how they are going to choose to react to them.

As soon as, you start to catch your thoughts, start to ask yourself, why am I judging them this way? By this simple thought alone, your thoughts towards others will start to change. I want to stress to you, that you need to catch your thoughts on everything, everyday, until it begins to become second-nature to you. It doesn't take long to achieve this. Within about one month, you can dramatically change these patterns of judgments. It generally takes years to build judgments, and can take only months, to reverse the process. Each time that you judge, stop and ask yourself, who am I to judge? Granted we are all co-creators with the same abilities as our God, but even our God does not judge, all of the experiences that each of us has had and will have.

God, nor Jesus will never, come down from the heavens, and judge people. This was another huge misunderstanding. Looking upward into the sky was a description given to the citizens of those past days to help them understand God and his powers. Citizens back then looked up to the skies for God, as many still do to this present day. Skies and heavens they could understand. Ask yourself, from a common sense point of view. Why would God, being that he is a non-judgmental God, come down from the heavens to specifically judge others? Wouldn't that be hypocritical? He is not going to come down and say you're right, and you're wrong. You will be saved, and you will not. That is blasphemy to me. It's one of those old theological scapegoats that we've all been exposed to, down through the ages. Once again, God will never do this. It is a fear-based concept handed down to keep us believing, and giving our money to the various fear-based religions.

Our own judgments are of our own making, or conceiving. That is why, we must release our false-judgments in order to understand, our true nature and being. If you want your questions of life, and understanding to be answered, you must release your judgments of others.

Politicians are very good in openly showing judgments, against their opponents. They're opinions of others judgments and just about all other opinions opposed to their own. Just like religions with all of their sects, and isms, of differing opinions. We all know everybody has different viewpoints and different backgrounds, so why judge them? To make yourself look better than your opponent, just for a job? Not a good path to follow.

One point that I would like to interject here, is the one concerning gossip and rumors. Why do a lot of people get excited over telling and receiving information, about other people? It is downright rude, and judgmental. Just remember this if you like gossip, and rumors, then you lack self confidence, in yourself. You are hearing and spreading words of gossip, to make yourself feel, and look better than another. Be confident in yourself, and your desire for rumors and gossip, will fall away. Through self-confidence, you will automatically start to judge others less, and your ego will diminish and no longer get in the way, as much. Be confident while expressing humility. Gossip is ego driven.

HOA's (Home Owner Associations) mostly, in the West, are based upon greed and selfishness. One neighbor doesn't like how another neighbor lives or the colors they choose to paint their house, or vehicles, trailers, RV, etc and it may be true, that the price of his house will drop. So rules are created. Why? It's all over money. You can't do this or that. More and more people are trying to find other areas to live in, to avoid HOA's. People are tired of being judged, and told what they can, and cannot do. This is what is also happening within the United States with bureaucratic laws, on everything. Those that can afford too will start to leave the United States, and live where they have more freedoms from laws. Granted the United States has a lot of freedom's and luxuries that most other countries don't, but the laws in trying to satisfy everybody, is greatly prohibiting that very freedom they have. Your home should be one of relaxation and peace. Not continued daily judgment, and added stress.

The concept of HOA's is how our laws and rules of society have escalated all because of others being greedy and selfish. HOA's have become a reflection of our society – the need to control each other. I'm still always amazed at stores, clubs, and organizations, and scholarships, who continue to remain exclusive. Exclusiveness is another form of a smack in your face, I am better than you judgment of others. Ask yourself, is this how I would like to be remembered, as know as being stuck up and being better than others around you?

Once you catch your thoughts on judging your fellow man, and you have figured out where your judgments are stemming from, try to release that judgment of that particular prejudice or prejudgment. For example, say you judge someone from their hair-style, or style of clothing. From that point on, try not to judge anybody, with that particular style which they enjoy for many of their own reasons, because it's flawed only to your opinion and perhaps to society in general. We must learn not to judge others, so we as a society, can reverse these trends, continually repeated in our society today.

Now, last but not least, let's talk about judgment of ourselves. We can be harder on ourselves. First of all, why? We, ultimately judge all of our actions and thoughts that we have, daily and in the end of our life. Learn to not judge your circumstances or your prior decisions. Become your best critic without being critical and/or judgmental to yourself. You must understand you have created your surroundings, including your physical and genetic make-up, to provide opportunities to experience, and understand. Your karmic lessons – Are very important for your growth and awakening. So embrace those experiences with those around you, for you have chosen them, to help you. Never judge yourself, in your abilities and physical or genetic make-up. Work with what you have.

Do not let society – influence your judgment of your appearance. It should not matter to you, one iota, what one would say to you, about your appearance. Ask yourself – who is he or she to judge me? It could be your parents, friends, teachers, and co-workers, whatever. Nobody can judge you, except yourself. You should know that within yourself; however, society is constantly tearing us down. Each of us is unique in our own way and there will always be somebody attracted to that. They see the uniqueness in it and really like it. I'm sure you have heard the phrase that there is always somebody for somebody out there. Now if everybody all looked the same then everybody is going to get tired of that very fast and your personality is still unique to you no matter how you change your body.

Also those closest to us can be the worst critics, however unintentional. They are simply trying to help you through their own judgements and mistakes they have gone through. They may apply to you or may not, but that is up to you to decide on and hopefully they realize that too.

I am opposed to plastic surgery, to enhance one's physical appearance. Be and become, happy within yourself. Everybody is different, and has their own abilities, and attributes, to contribute to mankind. What if your physical attribute was helpful to another to their understanding and you changed it? You look as you are because you chose that. Now you are using free will to change it which may bring a karmic tie with it.

Those who oppose, or put you down, you can decide to endure, or leave it out of your experience, entirely. Your choice! Be confident, and yet humble. Realize you create your destiny, and that nobody else can do it for you, unless you let them. For example, your lack of confidence in yourself puts you at the mercy of others around you, who are willing to use and abuse you. Remember, you should have complete confidence in yourself and know that, the only fears in your life are your own. Overcome your fear and others will see it and won't bully you. If they do then learn some martial arts and put them in their place. Bullies only go after those who feel weak in themselves. They won't dare go against somebody who is confident and strong. They can't handle that. It is perfectly fine to protect yourself.

If you are in a rut, ask yourself, is this what I choose to do? Some do, some don't. Be one that doesn't! Remember, to move forward, you must take action, or steps forward, to produce results. It's like the lotteries. You must buy a ticket to ever have a chance to win. If you sit back and wait for life to happen to you, it won't. You must get out there and take charge of your life. Your destiny is up to you! Don't compare yourself to others. Everybody has their own karma and circumstances, which will differ from yours. So don't compare, just live! Make your destiny with your own achievements, and then they will be all yours.

Remember, one is not greater than another! I bet if Jesus was before you, you would even put yourself down compared to Him? Why? Did Jesus not wash the feet of others and serve others constantly? He would not look at you as being lower than Himself. He would look at you as His own brothers and sisters. We are all here to help each other to experience our soul's awakening. Our awakening is as beautiful as nature herself is. DO NOT JUDGE OTHERS or you will be judged through yourself. Treat everybody like you would treat your own family. If they need shelter, give it to them. If they need food and/or money, if you have it give some to them. If not, help them get some money and/or food. As you would do for your family, do unto others. Life is so completely full of these types of opportunities. Take advantage of them. It will help all. Kindness and compassion crushes hindrance, thus breeding kindness and compassion amongst others. These two simple laws would change our entire world so dramatically and it can be achieved. Do not think of it as an impossibility. It is very possible. It will take time to reverse worldwide, but its effect will be felt and the momentum will continue. After 3000 AD to know yourself and you will know God will become the next awakening for us. But, we need to start this direction first. How can one even come close to knowing thine Father/Mother if one can't see another as the same as themselves? How can one know thine God if one continues to judge their brethren?

I read a small portion of a book the other day from a spiritual or inspirational leader the other day who wrote about Jesus' missing years. I was curious in his findings. It saddened me greatly. They were basically saying that Jesus' sayings could only apply if one was in the consciousness of oneness. It could not apply to our current and everyday living. We could not bring heaven to Earth and live the "Way," "The Pattern," without being in oneness most of the time. This is so wrong, backward and again a misinterpretation. Anybody and everybody can live in the "The Pattern" given to all without being in oneness. Living in this manner will bring about oneness naturally within oneself. "The Pattern" was given for this reason.

That consciousness or oneness is to know thine self to come to know and become one with God. The sayings I have given you have always throughout all time and in every realm there is, applied. Everybody has simply looked the other way to what we have all created and thus looked at these words as impossibilities that couldn't apply worldwide. Those are only excuses. They have and will always apply. If we followed the words given 2000 years ago and many times before this, our society would be completely different right now. But, out of fear, jealousies and judgments of others have created what we have presently.

I have been around since our origins on Earth. I have witnessed a lot. Those golden rules have been around then and still apply now and to the ends of our futures. They are very basic and very simple rules to live by. Nothing else matters.

Just imagine all of the money one spends on pampering themselves, overpriced clothing and all accessories, over priced metals, stones, expensive cars, big houses, makeup and all luxuries of life that we don't need. Just imagine how all of that money throughout the world would end all homelessness, starvation, illiteracy, deficits, massive research and development to cure all diseases scientifically, except for the one's that will always be ahead of science, good healthcare for everybody worldwide for free, unemployment and etc. Can you imagine this? It is all possible and realistic. We just need one really big push to start the momentum. Are you willing to help? Just shift your extra money from extras and luxuries to those that need the help. Don't worry about amassing wealth. You can't take it with you, so use it to help others. They will be more appreciative of your money than your family might be. I'm not saying you don't take care of your family, but there is limits. We all know this. Crazy thing, if you start giving away intelligently or in a certain pattern you will just keep amassing more wealth faster than you can give away and have even more to help even more people.

Just an idea! Just imagine!

The Law of Fear

Fear is the chief big obstacle to understand. Fear can be the biggest block to anybody's progression, in regards too, what they do in life. I could write an entire book just on fear. Remember, this saying. **What you fear, you will bring unto yourself.** I see this law in motion everywhere. It's the main driver of judgement. It is the biggest reason for spiritual failure, disease and illness. Remember, there is nothing in this world "to fear, except fear itself."

I see most people everyday living their life and making all their decisions based on fears. It's crazy. Not for themselves, but for fear. I just see fear dripping and oozing off of people like maple off of a maple tree. Poke a tube in them and the fear will be just pouring out of them just like maple.

What decision is the safest, which decision will give me less confrontation, which decision will keep me safer during the day/night, which decision is the safest for a job with security, I can't do this or that because I might get hurt or injured, which decision is best for the safest car or safest anything. I see fear just dripping off of people all day long and it is so intense. Fear will ruin your lives! You will never be able to truly live your life in happiness and freedom without getting rid of some fears. You will never be able to make a decision of what you truly would like to. It doesn't matter if it is safe or not. Will it make you happy and more enriched in your experiences? What do you want?

I could even compare living in fear is a lot like living in a regime or dictatorship. They make all the rules and punishments for you to follow. If you simply follow them then you can live your life in some kinda of fashion that is acceptable to them. If not, you'll know the punishments for it.

Fear is the root cause of spiritual separation, from our God. Fear can govern judgments towards others, relationships, jealousy, work, confidence within oneself, lying, failures, wars, depression, anger, frustration, addictions, power, greed, doubts, money, understanding, reactions to situations, shyness, violence, and personal appearance. Fears supercharge emotions.

We must understand FEAR, and thereby overcome, or control, its negative effects. Fear, why do we have fear? Fear is the emotional response to being afraid, of the unknown, security, confrontations and many other situations. Remember, it is an emotional response. It is only from our conscious mind – our ego. Fear creates so much stress in our lives. Why do we have fear? In some areas of our being, it is our primitive, built-in defense mechanism, of protecting our physical bodies and the people around us.

Forgiveness is the opposite of fear. In knowing this, we should have no fear. Our bodies are only used for us, to experience, the third dimension or realm of physicality for experiences and growth. Remember, if you want to truly protect yourself, release your fear. What you fear, you attract! Just like judgments!

So how are you going to use the body you have? Are you going to let fear, be the ruling emotion, of your body? Or are you going to take charge of your fear, and control your body? Fears can create a lot of stress on your body. Fears can breed illness and disease physically and mentally. Fears can be passed on through your DNA to your offspring. This is a very big question!

Look at most of the successful people in the present and past of this world of ours, in every aspect of life from spirituality to business. (Successful – meaning as the world has or currently views them as having achieved great knowledge and understanding in one or more area(s) of interest – not money). Fear has not ruled their lives. They created their surroundings, and took advantage of the various opportunities that came their way. A lot more individuals are born into very poor conditions of poverty, and end-up in the multi-millionaire plus status. Why? They chose to take control of their fears, and go for it.

I'll give you some straight up examples that I see in play, everyday, around people throughout the world. For example, you are afraid of being attacked, and/or raped. If you have an extreme fear of this, this will become so; it will manifest itself and happen to you. Remember, your mind is the physical creator – the creator is you. Thus, you create and attract your circumstances. Afraid of being killed, fear it enough, and it will happen. Afraid of being not being able to pay your bills and lose your home, fear it enough and it will happen. Afraid to talk to people, fear it enough and you will continually have situations that come up, that demand you to talk to people. Afraid of losing your children, fear it enough, and it will happen. Afraid of becoming handicapped or deformed, fear it enough, and it will happen. Afraid of falling or injuring yourself fear it enough, and it will happen. Afraid of taking tests and doing well in school, or your job, fear it enough, and it will become so. Afraid of being saved, or making it into heaven, fear it enough, and after you pass-on, you will feel and experience heaven is beyond your grasp. I say again, YOU will make it so. Afraid of your spouse cheating, and lying to you fear it enough, and you will make it so or will always be attracted to this type of relationships. Afraid of the opposite or same sex, fear it enough, and you will end up, alone. Afraid of disease and illness of any kind, fear it enough, and you will become sick. Afraid to get over your addictions and they will stick with you.

This thing about disease and illness, does concern me. You see, advertisers and doctors tell us take this or that to prevent future illness's and/ or diseases. What they don't realize, (which some advertisers/marketers do realize), is that they are implanting within your subconscious mind, that you will get a specific disease and/or illness, if you don't take certain preventative medicine(s).

Advertising can bring about some very unkind subconscious results. This is why, I am against advertising that is only promoting, negative thoughts within others. Science already realizes this, and yet they continue more than ever to create these very situations. Why? No-other than creating a fear in you, for their own monetary gain. Advertisers, salesmen, politicians and religions are very big culprits of this. Religion tells you, if you don't reform and change your ways, you will go to hell. Everybody knows already that they are not perfect, nor will they ever be up to religions standards. Therefore, you start to tear yourself down. You lose confidence; you believe you are not worthwhile and must be saved.

Big hint here: You are already saved! Religion is one subject that can constantly frustrate me, in how, and what they tell others, who are simply seeking legitimate spiritual help in their lives, and they can and do make it worse in a lot of cases! That is not a positive message for people, who are seeking spiritual help. They are breaking you down, and brainwashing you. Remember, what I see is a generalized or macro view of religion. Not all individual religions do these items that I discuss. You will have to use your own discretion about what is good and not good for you.

How many times have you seen medical science tell you some kind of food or medicine is bad for you, and then years later tell you that, they were wrong, and the body actually needs it? Or your doctor frightens you (intentionally, or well intentioned), by saying you have a disease or illness, in which, there is no cure or otherwise, and you have an "X" amount of time to live approximately? Whether the disease or illness is or isn't, they have implanted the seed in your thoughts that yes, you do have it, and thus your mind creates or speeds the disease or illness up. Or you choose to fight it and live on much longer than anticipated?

Why does medical science always use placebos? Because they realize how powerful our minds thoughts can be in influencing anything and/or symptoms besides the obvious cause and effect or baseline they need.

Or the classic religious ploy, preaches that it needs a certain percentage of your income, and if you don't your violating God in some way. It's not by accident that all of the sects and isms or religions, are always incorporating more sayings or acceptance of progressive world views to keep membership's full, and current with the times. What I am giving to you is the same Ancient Knowledge we all have, and it has never changed for millions of years.

Now, how do we reverse fears, when just like judgments, fear can take years to develop and yet within months, you can erase these fears. First, the faster you can accept that there is no reason to have fears, the faster and more successful and happier, your life will be. You will become in charge of your life and your decisions.

Make a list, of all your fears on any subject, situation, or thing you have experienced. Then pick the one's you want to rid yourself of, first. Start on the easy one's first for yourself. Then face it, maybe slowly at first, but remember if you face your fears head-on, you will eliminate them almost immediately.

This is how hypnotism works. Your subconscious can override the past fear, and so, the conscious mind has no record of past fear, and no fear is shown and/or felt. But, whatever you choose is fine, just take action, in doing it. Action towards it is very important. Let's use some examples – say, you have fears of heights. When you have the opportunity to face it, face it. Start with small heights, and then increase it until you no longer have the fear, or the fear itself will no longer stop you, in achieving what you are capable of.

Hint: as one example of; If you are absolutely terrified of heights, it probably has to do with a past life and you have fallen to your death. It's the past! It has followed you until now and will continue to follow you on other lives until you face it and get over it.

To help you, think of it this way, that this fear will not end my life, but only make me stronger. Same holds true even to bees or animals. I have watched this bee thing play on for decades watching people with them. Even kids have become afraid of them. Like I mentioned earlier, if you fear them they will come. You take somebody like me and I will work and play around them. As long, as I don't specifically go after them, they won't go after me. I do my thing and they do there thing. We live in peace around each other. Even wasps.

The objective is to not let fear stop you from achieving what you want to do. Some fears, I don't want you to confront, such as, injury to yourself or another, as in rape, and don't jump off a building trying to break your fear of heights and etc. Use common sense. With these you must first figure out why you are afraid of them? Being controlled and/or violated? It can be based on an experience in this life, or a previous life.

A lot of fears take lifetimes to accumulate and/or to remove. Remember you are given opportunities to understand and grow. Releasing fears, and karma, is the main reason for experience, and to grow and experience life, with spiritual unfoldment or awakening, this is why you are here. Is your fear of being a rape victim? Then learn a martial art in order to protect yourself. But remember, you need to lose your fear, or you will attract it to yourself. I can't stress this enough that you must get over your fears, or they will follow you, and you will live your life, as your fears' directs you. Your fears will follow future lives of yours and can be transferred to your kids through your DNA.

Another example that is so obvious to me that I see. It's a bully thing again. Look at shootings. Where is mass shootings done at? They are done at places where usually only innocent people who are not armed are at. This is a big and easy win for them. Everybody will just run away from them while they shoot. They win. They are the strong one. You will rarely see them say attack a military facilitate. Why not? Because there is a hug chance that they will be shot at themselves. They don't want that! They are afraid and basically bullies trying to make some point of how they were treated by others and taking it out on the people who can't harm them back so they can inflict the biggest reaction they can out of it.

Now I know you're thinking ok let's take all of the guns away? Yes, it will work to a degree. Pulling knives on others in mass does take a lot more courage to pull off and the reaction overall won't be near as big. So they might revert to explosives. You're not going to stop it until we start treating each other with respect. As technology progress's there will always be bigger options of this to play out against people. So don't be surprised when these things happen. We have created these exact situations to happen. I'm just surprised it has taken so long to get to this point.

If you don't like it then start changing how you deal with others. Show respect, caring and dignity. Treat everybody as if it was your own family and these problems will start to disappear. If we continue on like we are they will become commonplace to where we will all start to be armed to combat it. Like I have said many times now, bullies don't like confrontations that are equal or stronger than they are. They need the one's that are weaker than themselves to pull it off or at least, not armed so their chances of survival are a lot better because ideally most of them don't even want to be caught. They just forget to see the obvious in this day of age that there is a very high chance you're going to be caught.

There is nothing wrong with protecting yourself or somebody else if injury is happening or going to happen. Instant karma. Nothing wrong with that at all. I personally have very little tolerance for people who intentionally try to hurt others in any way. Whether it's physical, mental or even stealing from another. It's one of my flaws I guess or I've just been around it too much within all my lives that I'm sick and tired of it. So I have no problem with dispensing instant karma if needed. Maybe they will come to understand it next time they come back and won't do it again.

When your fears do catch up to you, you will have a split reaction, to react to it. That's your last chance to overcome it. If you don't, then it will repeat itself, again and again. Maybe not in this life, but it will happen again and again, until you get over it.

Fears will bring out your jealousies of other people. This is because you have listened to others, and brought your self-esteem and confidence down. Why? You have allowed others to judge you, think for you, and you have accepted their judgments, and agreed with what they have told you. Therefore, as you get older and mature, you have more doubts about yourself, and surroundings.

Why do you think older men and woman can act and say a lot of things such as cussing and get away with it. Because they have given up some of those fears and no longer care if people like it or not. They are simply being their real selves.

As your doubts increase, all of these little things like anger, jealousy, lying, etc., start to come out. With self-esteem and jealousy, it is that it has taken years to build, and tear you down, and the bad thing is, it will take usually a year or more, to recover your lack of self-confidence. Remember, anything you bring on in this life unto yourself or you're being, takes longer to recover from. It's a slower process to get back, because you judge yourself harder, and you must change yourself, and you're thinking, before you can start to change this. It's like an addiction, you must be all around others who will support you, and give you positive feedback, instead of negative.

The best thing that I can tell you to do is, tell the truth. You have to tell yourself that no one on this Earth, or elsewhere, can judge you, and know why nobody is better than you anyway. They aren't. They just have different circumstances. Nobody, not even the Pope, is better than you. We are all equal.

Nobody can judge you, unless you let them, judge you. Be confident and believe in yourself. If you get knocked down by life, which you will many times over and more, just turn around, and get up and start doing your thing, again. There are always opportunities given to you to grow and awaken spiritually.

If others judge you, then, through understanding, try to understand why they are judging you. Know that their judgment is, generally, based on fear. Look at their surroundings, and try to feel why, they are judging you. Through this manner you can learn from them, and feel empathy for them, which will lead to your understanding of them. Until then, don't accept their judgments, until you come to understand them. Once understanding is achieved, you will not pay attention to their judging of you anymore. You could even confront them now and tell them why they are judging you is out of their fears. They won't like that, but deep down it will reach into them and make them question themselves. That subconscious type of message is powerful. Then you will have officially freed yourself from their jealousy, and forgiveness can be solidified. Through understanding – forgiveness is given!

If people make judgments about how you look, ignore them, or better yet, look into their eyes for why they are saying what they are saying to you and understand why and then forgive, or say I forgive you. I know it is easier said than done, but look at it in this way. They are generally saying it is because they are lonely, or angry within themselves. So, they look for other people, who will accept their judgments or criticisms, about what they say or do (Bullies). If you ignore them, then their judgments have no power over you. You will always come out stronger spiritually. Also, think about it this way. What they judge, they will become judged later on through the same, or close to the same circumstances you were in. Thus, karma comes into play. Hopefully, they will come to understand this before, they judge themselves and that experience will be graced upon them.

I'm sure the lower economic status of others is questioned a lot from most of the population in our society. I'll tell you why and you might not like the answer nor believe me, but it is what I see.

People all over the world, including the middle class, fear that they won't and can't ever make enough money, or will be good enough and/or intelligent enough, to survive and pay their bills. If people would lose their fears of money, and accept and take appropriate actions to move forward, many opportunities to make more than enough money, would be given unto them. So obviously, there are a lot of people who fear money or the lack of it.

Churches should follow the same concept, but out of their fear, certain religions won't. They are fearful of failure and thus they demand through God that their, followers must provide for the Church, because God in the Bible has told them to do so, or they will be a sinner, basically. This is a perfect example of a misunderstood saying in the Bible or other religious book and has been rewritten by various religions for their benefit, and yet stems from such misunderstandings, thereof. Do unto others as you would have them do unto you, is what it breaks down to. The paying of actual money or dowry is not mentioned to be given specifically to organized religions. The giving to another is worded, and was intended to be given back to another for helping you and it wasn't money in the first place. It was helping each other back and forth with spiritual awakening. Like the pay it forward concept. Churches turned it into dowry, which then became tithing for even more money. Jesus as the pattern has never needed money nor had patience for those seeking money. What need does a soul need with money to survive?

Now here is an idea! If a church wants to become the biggest church of them all. Why don't you give each person or family 10 percent of their earnings to them? Will the families or individuals not prosper more? Not to mention you would have millions if not billions of people joining your church.

Another saying that is misunderstood is having a House of Worship. It was never intended to be an actual church or building. Yes people can congregate, but needed a church is not needed. The House of Worship is also misunderstood, and rewritten incorrectly. The House of Worship is the house of yourself, no particular place, just the individual. Each of us is our own House of Worship. Each of us hold our own Heaven or Hell within ourselves. Just as if you are praying. It is you yourself praying from yourself. You are the House.

So you can see that fear is a big thing in life, to most of society. Some religions are threatening (or brainwashing) using fear to induce you to donate. Some people have abused others with their money from before, and they must switch places now, in order to learn from their experiences. Some feel that they are not worthy to have money. Why? Because they believe it is greedy. There is nothing wrong with money if the ideal is correct. Actually, the more you receive, the more you should give out to helping others, and this doesn't always have to involve money. Money is simply an example of. Everybody has their gifts and talents, to give to others. I heal a lot, but most don't even realize it.

Another situation that I hear a lot of is that we as parents are always trying to give our children more than what we had hoping that their life will be better than ours. I have even said it myself. But, it is only an excuse of our own lack of self-confidence and security. Remember, our children want our moments, not our money. If they want your money, there is a problem there. Like I said earlier in this book, many very economically-challenged people have turned themselves into multi-millionaires. It was their choice, not their parents.

You can help anybody with what you simply have, which is what I like to see. It doesn't have to be money. When you're in the grocery store or out shopping, just be very courteous and kind to others. Don't be self centered to others, just be polite. In doing so, it makes everybody around you feel better. It is contagious. When you see somebody who needs some help, just help them. These are the little things that we can all do, to help each other out. In doing this, in time, others will be respectful to you in return from karma. It's a cool cycle that I do see here and there with others. You could also just help to volunteer for various causes.

Remember this hint: If somebody is rude to you, or angry at you for whatever reason, they call you names from road rage, poor cashier taking your anger or whatever it is. Always remember, this law of continued motion of karma and forgiveness. When one does this to you, in any manner opposite of being kind to you, don't get mad or emotional back at them. Simply say Thank you and have a good day! This drives emotional types of people crazy. But, that kindness inserts a seed into their subconscious and soul. They will continue to think about it and they won't be able to get it out of their head. Eventually, they do, unless somebody else hits them again with acts of kindness in return. But, eventually each time, each seed is shown and dropped. Eventually, they will show the same to others. Continue to be kind to all. Through kindness, emotions and egos of others start to reverse and fade away, until all are kind to each other. Kindness and patience creates understanding – understanding creates forgiveness for all.

Greed is another whole type of subject. Greed comes from abusing opportunities given to one and then abusing others with those opportunities. Whether they deprive others from their money, or keep more of the money for themselves, instead of circulating it to others, as in profit-sharing. Greed stems from the fear that one doesn't have enough to share with others, and/ or feels that one deserves most of the money, or opportunity given to them, and thus they deny others. Entitlement is an excellent example of such. Selfishness is an effect of greed.

Taxation in politics is a good example of misusing funds from everybody. If it is misused, governments will have to increase taxes to attempt to correct their flaws, which in turn, makes the general population very upset. Then government's start to run out of options, and almost has to turn into a government controlled society, to keep control of its people. We are seeing this more and more, in current times. So be very careful of taxation, and continuing restrictions of laws on individual's freedoms. This will eventually backfire. I keep hinting on this subject with taxes for a reason. I hope governments of the world are listening?

Hint: Reduce taxation to almost elimination of. How much money do you really need? People and businesses will use that money to grow and provide jobs, and then society will flourish. This is a massive and great challenge I'd like to give out to all governmental entities of the world. It will work; just decide to reduce your governmental size and control, but certain countries need to be aligned or rooted out first so there won't be wars in the future between countries. Reduce the number of politicians; rid yourself of lobbyists, greed and selfishness. Of course, this also applies to all big businesses out there. Be good and giving to others. Remember, your employees or workers helped your company get where it is, no matter the position. Remember, all are equal. No matter if you are the CEO or cleaning person.

Through greed, power is born. Greed deals more with selfishness, as power deals more with, control over others. There is no reason why one should be given more power over another. In the present and past, it was given to others, from the people, supposedly, for the people. Whether it was diplomatic, or through a tyrant's control. Power is a position that should be taken very gently. It is easy to abuse, and if your motives aren't of the highest, you will suffer, and eventually fail.

Most addictions are simply fears of dealing with life's confrontations and/or peer pressure. And the best way to conquer these addictions is to have the support of others around you that avoid addictions. The second way is through yourself. There is no magic pill, or easy way to get around it. Addictions are the same way we immersed ourselves into the physical in the first place. Like I said, addictions are generally caused from refusal to confront situations. So, you must learn to confront issues, and the best way in these situations, is head-on. This is why addictions are so hard to overcome. You are not allowed to run away from your problems. Once you accept and deal with your situations, then overcoming your addiction(s), will become much easier. Taking responsibility of your actions is also very important with addictions. You must be responsible for yourself, and then you can help others.

The same holds true with illnesses and diseases. One of your best defenses is your mind. Don't sit back and get depressed. Deal with it, and enjoy your life, this will do wonders for you. Your mind and body will help you to fight your disease or illness.

Anger. Anger comes from your being frustrated over lack of control. Taking what others tell you and agreeing with what others tell you, especially when they tell you that you are no good, or not good enough. Eventually, when you are constantly told you are worthless, and put down, your anger comes exploding out of you. This anger is your soul fighting back in your defense. It's trying to get you to wake up, and no longer accept what people are telling you, about yourself.

So anger is trying to re-establish your self-worth. It is a wake-up call, for you to stop taking abuse from others. Through understanding and patience, you can rid yourself of anger, and forgive those around you. Don't try to understand anger within yourself. Instead, figure out why others around you are triggering your anger, and through understanding of those answers, you will find peace and calm. Each time you figure out how to control what's triggering your anger, the stronger, and better, and calmer you will become. Hence, more control over your experience – yourself, not over others, and the happier each moment of life will be.

FEAR will bring FEAR! There is nothing to fear from FEAR! It's a made up illusion.

Prophesies

Since everybody likes prophesies, I will give some examples, I see here overall, in the world today into the future. Granted I wrote this in 1996 when I was 26. So let's see if I got some if it right. I didn't add anything to it for this chapter as I did add to my other chapters with examples with certain movies and more advanced insights.

I'm not going to give you a direct answer to global warming. It's pretty obvious. Once we hit the year around 1998 to 2000, and we still chose to ignore our environment, and the damage we continue to inflict upon the earth, thus onto ourselves, at this point, there will be no stopping the Earth changes that are presently coming our way. We now have to decide how long we want the supposed changes to linger on us. Two centuries or nearly three to four centuries or more?

There is no need for me to say anything more about this subject, except that our indulgences and how we treat our fellow man/woman are destroying our resources on Earth. We are not hurting the Earth. The Earth can easily take care of itself, but we are destroying ourselves through our greed and selfishness. Now the Earth can and will become more active to us. It is taking care of itself and we are simply a bystander to its forces that we have created unto ourselves.

Our Earth cycle should be a colder one right now, instead it is growing warmer, and will continue to do so at a pretty steady and fast pace, unless science can fix the ozone layer, or create a covering, like the ozone layer, to protect us. That can, at least, buy us some more time to fix it all. Science will be surprised how much the oceans are warming and will continue to do so.

We found fossil fuels convenient for our time and helped to advance us, but now we need to suck it back up, recycle what we have done or re-use it further and/or restore it within Earth or space. We need balance again. But, this won't happen for quite some time, which means, we will continue to get hotter, much faster than the scientists have predicted. Extremes of cold alternating too hot will be seen as more commonplace.

The oceans will also rise faster, than scientists have predicted. A lot of coastal bordering lands, states, and parts of countries, will start to be covered by water. Most will be partly covered while some almost completely. Rivers will rise, causing major flooding, much greater than we have seen in millenniums.

The storms we have started to see are only a glimpse, of the upcoming storms, hurricanes and typhoon's, that we will start to see and will increase every year or few years in number and size. We have some very massive hurricane's and tornadoes coming. Have you ever imagined a half country sized storms? Hard to imagine.

Volcanoes will start to become active in trying to release the inner heat and pressure. The volcanoes are still on hold, so to speak, depending upon our continued actions. Glaciers will become extinct before 2100 unless science can stop it. Possibly even by 2050 depending on our actions. I cannot emphasize enough the flooding everywhere! Mass areas of land turned into inhospitable areas like the deserts we have right now, but even hotter to the point you will die if you travel in these areas. Fires all the time even in winter months. The positive on this is all those areas that keep burning there won't be anything left to burn. Just turned into deserts, so to speak. Any island, South and North America, Europe, Australia, Italy, and everywhere where the land is not elevated enough will see substantial flooding.

As I continue to repeat, this is going to happen much much faster than scientists predict and will far exceed their predictions of storm strengths, flooding and heat. The world will have to be re-mapped from the changes. Science won't be able to stop this part of it fast enough. It is going to take some serious time to turn it all around. Not an instant fix. That bubble that I talked about will be the closest fix to instant that will buy us more time to fix things. Once things are fixed the bubble can be released. This is reality in the making I'm sorry. Now an ironic part to the global warming is that science will actually figure out weather and probably be able to maintain Earth climate around the 60s to 80's temperatures. Hawaii everywhere!

The answer to the pole shifts has been and will continue to move is caused from the balance of the Earth shelf. As more ice and glacier's melt, the increased melting shifts the weight of water throughout various areas. This balancing out, as in a scale let's call it, has distributed the water throughout, thus creating a calming or slowing of the wobble of our Earth. Soon it will reverse or create a different wobbling effect. The wobbling will continue on its angle until most of the melted water is evenly distributed. This is why the poles have been starting to shift.

This century is going to be very interesting for natural phenomena, and it can take centuries for our recovery. We have created these problems for ourselves, and have chosen to ignore them, and push them onto future generations. Well, as far those future generations - Now you have it - it's already here! We keep refusing to look at the big reasons of why, and we continue to push changes into other areas, so the big problems just continue on.

We are all so involved in our own being, and surroundings that we have chosen to ignore everybody, and everything else, thus, losing that connection where we are all connected together, as one. It's a price that is coming our way, and there isn't much that we can do about it, because we have intentionally ignored a lot of it, and greed and power, still rule over our treatment of the general population.

That's why I am all for more research and development, for alternative energy. These alternatives are a must. Do it now, while we can prepare better or deal with it, or we can wait until life and death struggle against the elements begin. Your choice? These alternative solutions have been around for decades, but always bought up, and hidden from us, because of greed.

Again, to science, look at gravity, magnetism, vibrations, lasers, and solar through crystal amplification. Plants only use so much photosynthesis for themselves because they can only handle so much at a time. Extra would be a waste for them to get rid of, but for us and science we can go way beyond plants for energy like photosynthesis. Even though our current technology is great, it is still far inferior to the inventions we have had in our past. Eventually, we will all have free energy through the air that surrounds us to power anything. It's not really the air itself, but the molecules in it. Technology and medical science will continue to grow exponentially, kind of obvious.

I've always wondered why we don't live under the ground versus on top of it. Maybe it's cheaper? Living below ground provides more stability, greater protection from the elements, provides better insulation and would solve a lot of our housing problems related to the natural elements of Earth. We have been using caves for millions of years for good reason when possible. We could always build a top floor with windows to see all of nature if that is the draw of it? Or perhaps it is an ego thing. Show off what you have?

In the United States, there is a good chance that our White House will be relocated and be built in Denver, Colorado, or Colorado Springs, Colorado because of its growing stability, central location, and it will be cheaper to rebuild than try to fight nature.

You see, our White House is going to have difficulties with water rising, as will other states and countries, as well. Everybody will be affected to some degree. England, Italy, Florida, California, New York, New Jersey, Louisiana, Japan, Texas, Australia, lots of islands and many other coast lines, are going to have some very serious problems with holding water back. Hint: You are wasting your time and resources on trying to hold back what is coming. You don't have enough time to stop what is coming.

There are a lot of future changes within our society that may come to pass, as in the humanity aspect. Psychic abilities will become more commonplace among people. Someday the way we conduct facts and evidence, for justice, will no longer be needed. Science with the help of psychics will discover the subconscious vibration that I and others have talked about. With all of this evidence down to every detail, crime cannot be hidden, and all will be exposed.

At first, it will be through other psychic's, who can touch up on this vibration, for evidence. As time continues on, the psychic's will no longer be needed to tap into this vibration, because science will finally figure out how to tap into the vibrational stream on its own, and it would be like observing a DVD in detail, of anyone's lives.

Wars should fade out of existence after 2100, at least the big world wars of devastating consequences. Governments will be decreased, due to technology, karma, and increased communication. Starvation and homelessness can be wiped out, if religions and/or private sectors, join together to wipe these out. Cars or cigar shaped vehicles will be flying, as magnetism and gravity is finally figured out. No more heavy lifting of anything not even your luggage once gravity is figured out through magnetism and wave manipulation. Teleportation will be possible, and star trek's science fiction of food replication, will become commonplace like the microwave is. This will come way before teleportation of ourselves. Food is just molecules put together in random ways.

Religion, as organized Churches will become extinct, or join as one big non-denominational religion. Don't let your egos and greed take center stage. I urge you greatly learn to work with each other with one ideal to help all the good of all. I cannot emphasize this enough. I will be watching to see if you can release yourselves from greed and become truly forgiven with grace. If not, karma will finish the job for you. Your choice!

We will stay here on Earth until 3465 or 3456. Then we will be leaving the Earth in mass, as we know it, and traveling to other planets, their moons and nearby galaxies to live on. In that year, we will start to be forced to leave the Earth.

In regards to science and technology, I cannot stress enough, how much they will advance. The things of the future that I see are hard for me to understand and explain. It is like seeing a computer with the internet for the first time, and trying to figure out what they are and their function and relationship are to each other. I keep seeing this invisible bubble around us that protects us but we move freely in it like it isn't even there and yet it functions as everything to us. With this invisible bubble we can travel, work, communicate, and have our leisure time. Everything we do can be completed within and through this invisible suit or bubble around us as if we are touching thin air for everything.

Within a decade or two the world will go through a major depression caused by big business greed, then politics will get interesting after that stage then you will see more rioting worldwide become more commonplace even within the US. Things you would never think would come to pass in the US. You will see with the politics, riot's and crime.

Beware, we have some very potent chemical and biological weapons or what science is trying to create let's say. I would be more worried of our biological getting accidentally released into our environments. Yes, others will try to use it as a targeted type of thing, but it's the accidental release we must be more worried about. Just too easy to spread amongst ourselves.

I am not a person of doom and gloom. I am quite the opposite. In that opposite of, I tell it as I see and feel it.

The great positives that I see, since over two thousand years since, is great strides in spiritual awakening. Un-paralleled strides of spiritual awakening greater than any other since our origins on Earth, a very peaceful feeling of calmness and rest. The momentum has begun and soon it will skyrocket and will continue to skyrocket and grow for many centuries. It's an awesome sight to finally see.

Through communication technology our separation of each other will reverse and we will all start to come together to help each other. This is good.

Our philanthropy has increased substantially in the last few years, which I salute all who help, but it hasn't seen anything yet. Over the next several decades, philanthropy will break all records since our origins on Earth. More and more of the upper class we have judged will be giving away more and more to all in their own ways. But, the ironic twist that I have mentioned earlier is that the more you give away the more you will receive to give away if done intelligently. Could last several decades or possibly more going out to others.

Do not trust the leaders of the Middle East, Iran, North Korea or Russia. China is borderline, but may fall into place with the majority of the countries. None of them are satisfied with what they have. They want more and to show the world how strong they think they are. They are not about peace! It is going to cause a lot of problems in the future. We will have to deal with these countries whether it is by force or otherwise in the coming decades.

I stress again, do not believe what they say. Like young souls who haven't experienced real consequences yet. They don't know better and think they are stronger and smarter than everybody else and will try to take what they want. They will test the limits of how the world will react to them. If the reactions are minor they will keep pushing the limits to the max eventually forcing other countries to react. Just like a child tests their parents.

I am going to be very blunt here: If we don't stop them it will bring much greater consequences and bloodshed to all. Sometimes, it is better to act forcefully and end things than try to be nice and drag the situation out. Bloodshed and destruction doesn't mean much to them, unless it's on their own land. Just like a bully, once you decide to confront them and go after them they will crumble. Like a child, sometimes it is better to take away their toys by any means necessary for the good of all. We all ready know how hollow they are and just like a bully throwing out empty threats in trying to maintain its strength that it realizes it doesn't have. These countries could be the last big wars we have left.

The way we deal with these countries will also determine how China will decide which way to turn. The more we drag it out the greater likelihood we will have to deal with China too. The faster and more forceful we are the greater chance that China will fall inline with the majority of countries to avoid worldwide confrontation.

Worldwide the upper economic structure that we all have judged will show its force and start to eliminate and solve so many plaguing problems in our world, such as starvation, most disease and illness, alternative energy sources (but this one will be a big struggle) and many other things. So many things. Someday a possible leveling of all will be possible.

Like I have said, earlier medical advances will soon be able to provide us with almost immortality before 2100. Making us almost disease free. After 2100 robots will generally take care of us instead of doctors. The robots will be the doctors fixing us. Just single scans of our bodies will show everything.

Science will soon discover in the next few decades what I have said about our body. Our bodies are incredibly strong, highly complex(far more than science has yet to understand) and resilient body building machines. Train our bodies to fight any disease and illness. Sometimes, our bodies get off track and need to re-learn what is good and bad for them just like the energy patterns I see. It could be a genetic code gone bad or missing and things brought on by our life styles. Our bodies can re-heal nerves, break down tumors, re-adjust glands for diabetes, even re-clean our pipes, rejuvenate our organs again and kick out excess waste and clutter that builds up. Look to ways to enhance this ability and progress in letting our bodies change things. It will go a lot faster than trying to change things externally and put them into our bodies, unless they are created from neutral stem cells or tiny robots. Surgeries into our bodies will become much rarer as these things are figured out. Surgeries would be used for emergencies, as they should be.

I dare say, eventually in several millenniums we will actually be able to break our bodies down and re simulate them back again with simple thought. Long gone will be the need for food or water. Just energy absorption is all we will need.

Science will discover everything needs to be recycled in this manifested illusion. Energy always needs to get recycled into a new form to rebuild again. Black holes are giant recyclers of energy themselves. They kick out energy and vibrations which then can re-create again. Everything in the physical breaks down eventually and gets recycled. So no matter how immortal we may become we too still need to get recycled, as well. Just one of the laws, we have put into place. Maybe we have realized it a long time ago that being immortal in the physical experience isn't necessarily a good thing for us. We still need to move on to experience more and other dimensions. Just because we are afraid to pass on is only an excuse of FEAR!

Science will have finally figured out this vibrational link I talk about and will be able to download your thoughts. Thoughts will be a lot more public to all. I have always loved all the subjects science. Free and unlimited power to all hopefully by 2100. Depends on how much fighting over trying to control that. Science will discover that there is faster speeds than the speed of light. Look at wavelengths. Light is still simply an effect from its source.

Famine and starvation for our personal selves will disappear once we figure out molecular manipulation and create a microwave type of contraption that makes it within seconds for us.

Before then we will find mass quantities of hidden ground water in the earth further down and will also be able to desalinate at an unlimited pace which is good because we will have plenty of water soon. A lot of scientific advances coming with the next 100 years. An exciting time.

I'll answer one question that I have seen as prophesy from others. This one about China being the cradle of Christianity. This has already begun with the Tao over two thousand years ago and actually has been around for very long time before that. Since the beginning of time for us. The Ancient Knowledge.

All of these upcoming changes and philanthropy will kick start spiritual awakening for many centuries to come.

Conclusion

At this time, I will say unto others:

- Judge and you will be judged. Help others.
- Know thy self and know God
- Do unto others as you would have them do unto you

In conclusion,

Once the knowledge and wisdom in this book is fully or close to being understood, the entire culmination simply leads us to these three truths, of our existence.

1) We are literally co-creators of and with God – as one with our source and connected to all and all realms.

2) Everything is a manifested vibrational illusion – Every realm or dimension, is simply another manifested vibrational illusion to our soul.

3) We are here to help each other, and through this helping others, we will fully come to experience ourselves, thus know God.

Final Thoughts

Behold our "Ancient History," can then become our future "Ancient Realms!!"

I send my Blessings out to all!

Samuel F McCord

www.ingramcontent.com/pod-product-compliance
Lightning Source LLC
LaVergne TN
LVHW010107170826
845678LV00012B/2272
* 9 7 9 8 8 4 9 6 5 3 9 5 2 *